THE WIFE SWAPPERS

THE WIFE SWAPPERS

BONNIE GOLIGHTLY

CUTTING EDGE

ISBN-13: 978-1-962896-76-4

Published by
Cutting Edge Books
PO Box 8212
Calabasas, CA 91372
www.cuttingedgebooks.com

PART ONE

CHAPTER ONE
MRS. GRANNIS

PEGGY GRANNIS was altogether startled by this man—*delightfully surprised* was too mild a cliche. And though the meeting had taken place an hour and two martinis ago, Peggy couldn't believe it.

Now he was once again helping her into his white Triumph (top down, lovely summer night, the works) and, still grinning to himself over something she had said, apparently hitting his private funny bone on the mark, he got in beside her and started the engine.

"What did I say that was so amusing?" she asked.

"It wasn't anything you said. It was how you said it. I liked it. The way you asked, 'Are you married or divorced?' Very direct."

Peggy smiled, feeling foolish and flattered. "I'm sorry," she told him, as at last a token apology was in order to this fascinating stranger. "I wouldn't have asked except you kept using 'I' and 'we' interchangeably."

"Well, to answer your question," he said with his smile that Peggy had instantly classified as charming, "yes, I am married. My wife and children are in Colorado for the summer. Colorado Springs. My wife comes from there. Her father used to be lieutenant governor of the state."

This piece of gratuity Peggy found slightly embarrassing and a little pathetic: offhand yet onhand, naive, pompous, pointed as a name-drop, yet as sad as tears. And it was not the first unnerving one of its kind in the hour they had known each other. She sincerely hoped there would be no more, for it would be a pity for disillusion to move in where charm so lay couched.

"I don't know Colorado at all," she murmured in uncomfortable reply to his statement, and barely listened as he talked in obvious enthusiasm of Pike's Peak and mountain climbing. He had managed to work his way to the Matterhorn and his first expedition by the time she tuned back in, but by that time it was too late; she was hooked.

It had all started that morning when Joan had called from Easthampton and suggested that Peggy hitch a ride out with one Ernest Marvin, also invited as a week-end house guest. "You won't like him, though," Joan had added after giving Peggy Mr. Marvin's office telephone number and a few other vital statistics.

"Honey, who gives a damn?" Peggy had laughed, amused though slightly exasperated. "What do you think I'm looking for—a summer husband?"

"Of course not," Joan responded. "But I just wanted to warn you. It's a long ride."

At the time, Peggy had wondered if Joan were being psychic, or if too many naturally suspicious minds had been airing themselves on the subject of Tom Grannis' prolonged stay in England. Then Peggy assured herself that it was her secret and Tom's that their marriage needed a rest to avoid a breakdown, and she immediately picked the phone up again and called Mr. Marvin.

Yes, Joan is right, she thought after arrangements had been made. Ernest Marvin, with his precise slightly foreign accent, sounded prissy, spinsterish and sixty. What a bore that ride was going to be.

So when six o'clock arrived Peggy was nearly felled by the masculine sight that met her eyes upon opening the apartment door. He was not sixty; he didn't even appear to be thirty. There he stood, a dark slender arrow of a man-boy, clad in his light summer suit, his beautiful black hair beautifully in place, his beautiful classic nose and mouth as precisely joined (as all of him seemed to be) as the precision in his telephone voice. And over one eye he wore a black patch. The other, large, gentle and very black, gazed at her fixedly, as if at an enemy. But once she had recovered herself, had asked him in, she realized that Ernest Marvin was merely extremely formal and liked to be restrained.

Yet he didn't. After he had helped her into her light coat and picked up her week-end case, he made some terrifically acute and yet whimsical remark—what was it?—about what the wind would do to her "nice yellow" hair in his open car if she didn't take along a scarf. Something about running through it barefoot. She couldn't reconstruct it. But it had delighted her; however he had phrased it, it had a real wallop of little-boy enchantment, edged somehow with sex appeal.

She was quite excited when he suggested that they stop off for a drink, literally one for the road. "—and we'll call Joan and Bill and tell them not to wait dinner on us," he added slyly.

Peggy gave him a sharp look and saw then that his sense of humor had been responsible for this remark, for of course no one in his right mind could expect any hostess to provide more than a midnight snack at the late hour they were due to arrive. Peggy felt all the more gay.

Her pleasure and approval continued at his choice of a place to drink. "The Renaissance!" she exclaimed. "I love the Renaissance. When Tom and I lived on 49th—or rather Mitchell Place—we always went there."

"I used to live on 49th Street myself," he replied, and, added cryptically, "up until a year ago."

This was the beginning of Peggy's confusion about Mr. Marvin's marital condition. After they parked the car and went inside the elegant little bar-restaurant, his conversation with its mixed I's and we's completely mystified her. But it was not until they were actually getting back into the car that she blurted out what was on her mind: Was he married? It was a pity, Peggy was thinking, looking now at his unbelievably perfect profile and reminding herself that she really should pay attention to his talk. She felt refreshed for her thought. So she could still feel; she wasn't dead emotionally yet, as Tom had implied. She still could be very very interested in a man. Maybe she did need a summer husband. But did Ernest Marvin, this rare and lovely combination of deft wit, good looks, rather absurd little-man dignity which, all the same, she could not help but respect—did Ernest Marvin need or want a summer wife?

CHAPTER TWO

BEFORE THE night was out in any event he had one; at least temporarily. It was the first time Peggy had had a one-night stand in years; she had given up such recreation long before she and Tom had been married, and that was four and a half years ago, almost exactly. She was absolutely amazed at herself, at her own inventiveness as much as at her desire, as she sat beside him in the car planning the whole thing. And the plan began really when she was in the ladies' room in the restaurant in Smithtown. As she was combing her long blonde hair (the wind had indeed run through it barefoot, scarf or no scarf), she heard Ernest say, apparently to the waiter, "The lady would like a very, very dry martini with lemon peel." A real noticer, she said to herself. That's what I like. A man who quietly watches everything. That one eye is keen enough for more than two. So when she returned she gave him what she hoped he would find to be a dazzling smile, and thanked him warmly for having remembered it was a martini.

With dinner he ordered wine, the right one, of course, and when they got back in the car they were both a little drunk, pleasantly so. All of which is going to make it easier, she thought to herself as he helped her in, warmly aware of his hand on her arm. Was his touch now more intimate, or did it just seem so because she wanted it to be? Her question was answered when he slid in beside her: he kissed her. Lightly, but there was something more than friendship there. And even in his voicel slightly lowered, as he said, "I like you," sensuality hovered, however delicately. To

Peggy it was a faint whiff of the headiest of perfumes. Presently, as they drove along, he took her hand, clasped it in his. The pressure was at the same time a little-boy tightness, fierceness, a sealing of friendship, and something more. Ineffably more. Peggy felt slightly faint.

"Want to stop off and have a nightcap with some friends of mine?" he asked.

Peggy turned in surprise. "Do you know a lot of people out here?" Then she felt slightly ridiculous. Why shouldn't he? She and Tom knew a great many themselves. "The reason I ask," she went on lamely, "is that I'm surprised we never ran into each other before."

"Betsy and I used to live out here," he said, smiling. "I thought you knew. That's how we know Bill and Joan. In fact, Betsy had a house out here before we were married. We sold it two years ago when we moved to Montclair. Easier to commute."

"Oh, oh, I see," Peggy nodded. "Then Betsy Sinclair is Betsy Marvin."

"That's right."

"Joan's roommate at Bennington."

"Right again."

"And I met Betsy a long time ago—at the beach. Coast Guard Beach, I think.' She mused for a moment, then in an effort to keep a note of sadness from her voice, said, "She's very attractive."

"Thank you. Yes, she is."

Peggy thought, yes, attractive, but I couldn't stand her. In the first place, in those days Peggy had been newly married with a vengeance and scornful of any woman who took the married state so casually as to retain her maiden name, even if it was for professional reasons. Besides, who ever heard of Betsy Sinclair, ballerina, even if she had had a slight success at City Center? Anyway, she had given up her career when her first child was born—given up her dancing career, and had taken to walking on other people's toes instead. It had made Joan unhappy, but she had agreed that Betsy could be quite arrogant. Most of the unpleasant impression Betsy Marvin had made on Peggy had been due to the way the woman complained about the high wind that day which was blowing over the beach umbrella, thus exposing her fragile loveliness to the unwanted elements. She had done so imperiously, almost paranoidally, as if the umbrella did it on purpose. Later Peggy had remarked that anybody with that vampire complexion had no business at the beach, even if her figure was well worthy of exhibition.

Betsy Sinclair Marvin had been, Peggy recollected, almost totally unaware of Peggy's existence that day on the beach. Peggy was hurt. Not only was she unaccustomed to being ignored, but she had looked forward to meeting Betsy Sinclair, Joan's roommate, the wild, wonderful brilliant one she had heard so much about. After that first meeting Peggy never saw her again. And Joan tactfully stopped mentioning her.

Now here was her husband—wouldn't you know he would be *her* husband—and here Peggy was, half mad in the head about him already. Planning a campaign. Should she stop, now that she knew all this? Going on seemed really immoral—vengeful, bitchy. But when he pulled up in front of a clapboard house on the road to Springs and said, just before kissing her again, "This is where my friends the Adams live," Peggy was really gone.

CHAPTER THREE

A S IT turned out, Peggy knew the Adams, too, though slightly. "Hi, hi," Charlotte Adams greeted them, and said to Peggy, "what a nice surprise to see you again!" as she opened the screen door on the front porch. "How's Tom?" she continued, then to Ernest, "Good ole Ern, thanks for bringing Peggy along. But don't tell me Betsy and the kids have left for the summer? I thought it was too cold for her out there before July. Or did you pack her off on purpose?" She gave Peggy and Ernest a joint look of mischievous implication.

"On purpose," Ernest replied in the same spirit, but Peggy wondered if she didn't detect just a note of prideful promise in his answer. Then Charlotte Adams' husband, whose name Peggy couldn't remember, was greeting them, shaking hands first with Peggy, then with Ernest, a man-to-man clasp of fondness, and they were being settled down and asked what they would like to drink.

After the drinks were served—Ernest insisting on making Peggy's himself—it became rather clear to Peggy that there were, in effect, only three people in the room, and she was not one of them. The rekindled fires of friendship had blazed up quite naturally, as they always do, and, however "nice" they found her, she was outside this glowing wall. Their talk all centered on mutual friends, all of whom, for some odd reason, Peggy didn't seem to know. She began to feel as if she had just arrived from some remote foreign country, equipped with a perfect knowledge of English, but no subject to use it on. Presently the whole thing began to bore her, and she gazed abstractedly at the "friends," considering them objectively, each in his turn, as one does a fellow passenger. When her study came to Ernest, she was overwhelmed with a great sadness, a nostalgia almost, as if she considered someone she had loved and lost.

It was then that the sadness froze into solid bleakness for the conversationalists were getting down to tacks: the talk was exclusively of Ernest's wife and family. The note of pride she thought she had detected earlier in his tone, a presuming but prideful possessiveness of her, now bloomed there for his wife Betsy, so much so that it struck her as appallingly ugly, like greed. She felt sick and probably looked it, for mixed in with repugnance for his husbandly pride was Peggy's own avarice: envy of Betsy's possession of him, her status as legal wife. *Her* conquest, if any, was over, gloriously won.

Instantly, it seemed, Ernest acted. Before she knew it, he was bending over her, his golden brown eye huge with tenderness, and he was saying, "Sweetie, you're drinking dregs. Why didn't you say you needed another drink? Or would you rather go?"

His solicitousness of her was so flagrantly sharp that her delicious sensation of enjoyment was almost smothered by discomfort. But a look at the Adams disclosed no signs of ill ease on their part. Instead the touching little scene seemed to amuse them, and Mr. Adams even said, "Ernie, boy, you sure know how to handle 'em," and he nodded his head in admiration.

Peggy, thus compromised, said yes, she thought she'd like another drink. And as Ernest himself again insisted on doing the honors, she wondered many things about him: what antenna, what prescience had signalled to him at the precise moment of her unhappiness at its keenest? How could anyone be that sensitive, that "noticing?" He had jumped up exactly when she had known she couldn't take it any longer, and he was there at her side. What did he care whether she was miserable or not? He barely knew her. Or had her own behavior been so obvious that she was already incriminated? Whatever it was, it was uncanny, and potentially dangerous, like having an affair with a mind reader.

But as he handed her her martini, wearing his "created-especially-for-you smile," Peggy knew that the lunar pull was as strong as ever, despite his rather vulgar and certainly shocking proprietary hovering over her. She wondered if the Adams thought an affair between them was in full progress. Mr. Adams' comment would seem to indicate the latter, or even be the utterance of the faithful husband whose own fidelity renders him blind, as well as smug, to the seriousness of flirtations on the part of his friends. Yes, Mr. Adams seemed to have been complimenting Ernest on being a "ladies' man" merely, and perhaps Mr. Adams was right; perhaps that is all it was. Or, considering their indulgence in general of Ernest's quite outrageous behavior—he had name-dropped like mad, had certainly preempted the tasks from them that etiquette required them to assume, not to mention the fact that he had barged in on them without warning, dragging along a friend—didn't all this tolerance mean more than their abiding fondness for him? Weren't they a little thick-skinned to put up with all this? Whether it was indeed the fast glue of friendship or just permissive sloth, she couldn't tell, but she was fascinated by the whole thing.

Once again in the car, and on their way to their final destination, she said, culling from what she had overheard at the Adams', "I gather that you and Mr. Adams are both in advertising, and that you were also New Jersey neighbors?"

Ernest confirmed this and went on to say that he and Hank Adams used to be in the same agency, that Hank had more or less gotten him his job. "They are practically our closest friends," he said. "It was because of them that Betsy and I decided to buy a house in Montclair—if we want to come out here in the summer we can always stay with them, or with Joan and Bill. Betsy was all for keeping our Easthampton place, too, but I pointed out that I just don't make that kind of money—of course her family is rich as hell, but I'm not. Besides, since she has to make her annual visit with Daddy in Colorado, what was the point?"

Peggy looked at him thoughtfully. Did she detect a note of snideness, downright bitchiness, concerning Betsy or was this just an airy, childishly candid statement of fact? One thing was certain—or rather several things were, built in upon each other like Japanese inrow boxes—Ernest Marvin was fiercely, beamingly possessive of his wife, however harshly critical he might be of this wife who happened also, by odd coincidence, to be a person; and the other certainty Peggy knew within this major certainty was that he might estrange or absent himself from the person Betsy Sinclair, but from the wife Mrs. Ernest Marvin, absolutely never. Leave you ever, divorce you never. What a marriage if that was the case.

And what a future she Peggy Grannis might have in store for herself! It almost made her catch her breath. It could very well be that she was eagerly, masochistically hurling herself toward Back Street.

CHAPTER FOUR

"Y OU DON'T seem very gay, darling," Ernest said and reached over and touched her, to her surprise, on the knee.

"I'm just sleepy," Peggy lied with a small false yawn to underwrite it, "and a little high."

In fact, she was anything but sleepy, but the inappropriate after-dinner martinis had hit her, and these in the heady company of desire for him, heightened everything while paradoxically seeming to deaden everything at the same time, like a drug. Now, under his touch, she felt her emotions fairly hum. But the part of her thinking mind that was still capable of conjecture remarked upon what a nerve he had, putting his hand on her knee, taking it all for granted. Then quietly the hand was lifted and he retired into silence.

Dimly it occurred to her that it was a hurt silence he had entered, or rather retreated into. He had taken her answer as a rebuff. Quickly, passionately, she put her hand on his arm, and when he reached up to give it an acknowledging squeeze, her head fairly reeled to his shoulder. Yes, it was all going to be all right.

When he had parked the car and before they entered the house, they turned to each other in simultaneous ardor and embraced. No matter what happens, she silently assured herself during the kiss, tonight we are going to go to bed together.

It was Peggy, womanlike, now sure of success, who broke away, patted her hair, and said while further adjusting herself, "We'd better go right in. The house looks pretty dark."

"Joan and the kids may be asleep, but ole Bill will be up."

Again the proprietary manner.

"Oh, he will, will he? Mr. Know-it-all," she teased.

"Yes, he will," Ernest said, and gave her hand a playful twist.

She was instantly reminded of someone she had not thought of in years: her first husband. So that was the attraction. He, too, had had a whimsical sense of humor, and they had lived that one year of their marriage when she was eighteen like frolicking babes in the woods. Was there also about Ernest something that was like Tom? She hoped not.

Then there was Bill standing in the doorway, the light from the hallway, just snapped on, casting a lemon velvet triangle on the dark masses of shrubs and grass. "Well, hi, you two. Where have you been? Joan gave you up for lost. She's gone to bed, in fact." He took Peggy's suitcase from Ernest's hand, while Ernest, slightly out of breath, explained about the too-leisurely dinner, bad traffic, and the spur-of-the-moment visit to the Adams.

Bill Roche was not handsome, but his solidly built good face had been all geniality as they entered, but once in the light of the living room after one look at the pair of them it changed. He looked distinctly worried. My God! thought Peggy. He *knows!* His voice sounded almost stiff—angry?—as he went about the routine of asking what they'd like to drink.

Ernest and Peggy casually sat themselves upon the living room couch, and as Peggy looked at Bill's turned back as he made the drinks, she thought: will it be that bad if we go ahead with this thing? Why? It's nothing serious, just a dalliance. But Bill had always been something of a prude, and, further, Peggy was sure that Joan and Bill were completely loyal to their marriage vows, maybe because they were truly devoted or perhaps out of fear. Who knew? In any event, she thought, I shall be discreet. But that did not preclude persisting. After all, I have nothing to lose. He would never tell Tom, and he probably won't even hint it to Joan. But it was a rather ludicrous situation—all of it—here among so many people that they both knew. Low French comedy in America.

Bill had one drink with them and lost no time getting out of their way. He paused briefly at the steps to say, "You're in Kathy's room, Peggy. You know the one, to the left as you get upstairs."

Peggy nodded, and Ernest said, "Never mind about her bag, William. I'll carry it up for her."

Bill's good night was almost feeble.

The minute his footsteps stopped on the stairs, Ernest reached for her, and they quietly, rather conspiratorially kissed. They grinned at each other after that and both giggled a little, looking at each other, holding hands. "He knows," Ernest murmured, in wicked triumph.

"Yes, he certainly does."

"Poor ole devil."

"Why poor ole devil?"

"He wants you for himself. He's jealous."

"I never noticed," Peggy said rather wide-eyed.

"Well, I saw you last!" he exclaimed joyously. Then, "Shall we? ..."

He almost extended his arm, as if in invitation to the waltz; or again, on dancing-school level, as if he had said: May I kiss you? Too shy-making, really. Too little-boy. A man takes a woman, a la Lady Chatterley's friend, and no minuets about it. It nearly put her off, but she had come this far....

"Yes ..." she said, as he led the way to his quarters, and she remembered that for all his braggadocio, he was really shy; for all of his restraint he was really brazen. Poor, dear, lovable thing.... What could Betsy have been like, not to teach him, or insist upon, soul-kissing as an expression of passion? For, Peggy realized now, admitting it to herself for the first time, that the brace, or two braces, of kisses they had exchanged had been, whatever else they were, as innocent of communion as lacy valentines. This man-boy was a master of tenderness, and tenderness does not necessarily imply fire....

Therefore, smiling to herself as she followed along—they tiptoed, of course—she thought of ways to shock him. The first thing she did when they reached his room and he turned on the light was to immediately begin undressing him and herself at the same time. She did so with a "wanton, gay abandon"—her own accompanying mental description of her dramatics—despite the full light, the unlowered shades, the possible amazed entertainment of the Roche's neighbors. But he seemed to like it. They giggled and scratched at each other as their clothes came off, and shortly there he was ... breathtakingly beautiful with his golden-tan skin, like a bronze of an Oriental idol.

"Darling, you're so pretty," he murmured breathlessly, kissing her ardently.

Peggy could feel his heart thud as passionately as her own as they lay down together on the narrow bed, as unmindful of the skimpy size of their bridal couch as though it had been their common grave. They lay locked tightly in each other's arms for a moment, their eager hands caressing, stroking, scratching, and then he took her with sweet passion—manly, yet tender, practised, yet restrained, sincere, yet casual.

When he lay down beside her, Peggy moaned, and realized that she had—that they both had—during the entire course of their lovemaking. Crying aloud in ecstasy was a rare bliss for Peggy. In fact, she had never had anything like it.... By contrast, all other lovemaking in her life had been clear-cut, definable, to the point. But this, this shining, shattering prism—what was it? She felt like a wild bird, set free. She reached over to stroke him gratefully, lovingly; she had given to him the full gift of Peggy Grannis—total, committed, involuntary....

He took her hand from his body, gave it a small squeeze and said, "We made a lot of noise, didn't we?"

CHAPTER FIVE
MR. MARVIN

B RIGHT AND early Ernie Marvin briskly awoke. He noted with cool interest that she had left her bra and a red scarf on his chair and immediately threw them into his own suitcase, for future, clandestine disposition. She had been pretty woozy when he had guided her upstairs, complete with luggage, last night, but she hadn't been a bad lay. Maybe alcohol improved her performance. Ernie was always suspicious of girls with her coloring—too blonde, too light—and her build. They were usually as frigid as they looked. Sex with her had been the furthest thing from his mind for the first hour or two after they had met. He supposed the idea really occurred to him during dinner—wine on top of Scotch sours always made him a little giddy. She was rather pretty, with an obviously good body, and maybe she would prove the exception in the frost department.

Maybe. It was too soon to tell. He dressed quickly, as he thought all of these things, and finally meticulously fitted the eye patch over his blind eye and assayed himself in the mirror, satisfied, as always, with what he saw. He had a right to be satisfied.

He left his room, after having made up the bed in his usual swift, competent fashion (and not due to Army training either; he liked things that way), and went down the hall to the Roche's sunken living room. Too early for anybody in *that* family to be up—even the kids—he thought in detached scorn as he continued out the front door. He started his car and roared out of the drive-way, bound for the Adams'.

Charlotte was in the kitchen munching toast and reading in her customary absorbed fashion when Ernest strolled in. She looked up and smiled at him, yawned and stretched. "Yum, yum," she said with a wink.

"Are you commenting on the toast?" he asked.

"Some toast," she said pointedly. "How was she?"

"Wouldn't you like to know."

"Certainly. I would, Hank would, everyone would."

"Well, nothing like you, sweetie. What are you reading?"

"A novel called CIRCLES, but don't change the subject."

But he disregarded this, and said in his quiet, authoritative manner, "Where's Hank?"

"Out on the tennis court with Appleton."

"That fag? Don't tell me he's here for the weekend again."

Charlotte sighed indolently, then nodded. "But not here, baby, if that's what you mean. He's staying with some of the boys down the road. Want some breakfast?"

Ernie gave her a sour look, as if the subject of Appleton had turned his stomach. "Just orange juice and coffee."

"No French toast, even?"

"No French toast, even," he said with a little playful smirk, his mood melting.

As Charlotte Adams moved from ice box to the stove, getting his juice and coffee, he followed her progress admiringly. She had a nice bottom, and those terrific legs.... "You ought to make it a point to live in shorts," he commented, and as she came to the table where he sat, he ran his hand up her leg until it was inside her shorts.

"Don't do that, sweetie," she said huskily.

He smiled, and continued to caress her, watching her eyes as they filmed with aroused desire. "Why not?" he said. "You like it, I like it, so what's the harm in it?"

"I'm too busy," she said, breaking away from him with some effort on her part. However, she lingered still within reach. "I've got the marketing to do, and the spare on the Jeep is flat."

"Why don't you let ole Hank take care of that?"

"He's busy too."

"Yeah. With that Appleton character," he said with sarcasm.

"Now, don't start that. You know Hank's no queer."

"I wonder."

"Well, *you* ought to know."

"Just because I've shared his wife in the same bed? That doesn't prove anything."

"Well, *I* can tell you, honey, he's great."

"Better than I am?" he asked in his little-boy teasing manner, just to beguile her.

She was properly beguiled. "Stop begging for compliments," she said with a crooked smile.

He looked at her thoughtfully and at the same time placed a bland smile on his own face for protection. Ole Charlie was certainly a pushover, always red hot. Why did she find him so irresistible? Was he particularly so, or was it just that she panted for anything in pants? Judging from Hank, he wouldn't have thought she'd go for his type at all. But big women liked small men—did he ever know that!—only Charl didn't strike him as the motherly sort. Never knew. For that matter, why had that Grannis woman developed the hots for him in first look? He wasn't complaining, mind you, nor particularly surprised, but ...

"Are you sitting there planning another sexual assault on me—or is it on that Grannis dame?"

"Neither, darling. I'm thinking about citified things, like will we get the Caravan account, like should I take another apartment this fall—"

"Oh, do!" she exclaimed, her eyes lighting up.

He grinned at her mischievously. "I just might, now that I've met Peggy Grannis."

"You will-o'-the-wisp, you!' she scolded him. "First you run her down, say she's just so-so, and now you're planning a love nest with her."

"Who ran her down? I didn't say she was 'just so-so'; you did."

Charlotte looked a little peeved. "Well, take the apartment anyway," she said.

"I promised Betsy I'd be a good boy next year."

"You promised Betsy you'd be a good boy next year," she said mockingly. "What's that supposed to mean?"

"Well, I did," he said innocently, and gave her a smile to match. "After all, Betsy is my wife. I owe her something."

"Oh, come off it, Ernie!"

"You know how fond I am of Betsy."

"I know you," she retorted. "You don't know what you are."

"I do, too," he said in a lazy good humor. "I know I'm fond of you."

"Go on, flatterer, finish the sentence. You took an instant fancy to me because I reminded you so much of your wife."

"Well, it's true."

"How come you don't sleep with her then?"

"Who said I don't? Of course I sleep with her."

"I don't mean share the same bed, sadist nut."

"Betsy doesn't think I'm a sadist. She understands perfectly. That's what I like about Betsy. She understands everything."

"That's more than I can say."

"Yes, I know."

Charlotte sat down and looked at him appraisingly. "You know, Ernie, sometimes you go too far."

"Like when?" he asked, still teasing, and put his hand on her bare leg.

"Like now," she said huskily, pushing his hand away.

But Ernie knew she didn't mean it, and grinned at her knowingly. "Shall we ...?" he said.

"Okay," said Charlotte. "But honest, I've got a million things to do today."

CHAPTER SIX

L ATER, THEY drove to town in tandem, or, as Ernie put it, they continued their "togetherness," because Charlotte had to leave the Jeep at the garage to have the starter fixed, along with the spare, and Ernie said he would take her shopping and drive her back.

He smiled to himself as he followed just behind her. Good ole Hank. "What have you two been up to?" he had called from the tennis court as they drove off, and when Ernie called back, "Just the usual," Hank had said, "Oh, that. Don't you ever get enough, fella?" Yes, good ole Hank. But he wouldn't want to be in Hank's good ole shoes. The sporting life would lose its savor for him if it included cuckoldry. A depressing thought; the same kind of letdown he'd felt when he discovered they'd let women into one of his clubs. But Hank there believed in the equality of women. The only woman Ernie had ever met whom he considered his equal—or better—was Betsy. And then on certain levels only. However.... He sighed and thought of his kids. He missed them. The house was so empty. Another six weeks.... But why not look around for an apartment before Betsy got back? He'd been joking, of course, about Peggy Grannis, but there was Charlotte, not to mention a handful of others....

He suddenly swerved sharply to avoid a large beach ball which a little boy in swimming shorts had accidentally rolled into the middle of the road.

"Sorry, Mr. Marvin!" the child cried.

"Hi, there, Jimmy," Ernie said recognizing the boy and slowing. "That's okay."

Yes, I love kids, Ernest thought. Charlotte loved kids, too, she said. Couldn't have any (Betsy couldn't have any more either). But was it really Charlotte, or was it ole Hank? Was he really a fag, or a bisexual? All right, so Ernie had seen him screw her. That meant nothing. Maybe he just had a hangup on that one dame, no other. For in all of their man-to-man talks, Ernie had never heard Hank contribute much to the topic of women. But then, he, Ernie, could pretty well dominate that subject anyway. Even if he had had a late start—he was twenty when that cute little Italian chick had showed him how. And if it hadn't been for another babe he wouldn't have caught that sniper's bullet. Suzanne de Vuillons. Of course losing an eye for a broad wasn't worth it, but if he hadn't pushed her out of the way, she would have had it. Anyway, in those days he had been a brave fool. It took Korea to get him over that. I've spent all my days fighting and making love, he thought—not without satisfaction.

Ernest Marvin was half Swiss and half American. He had grown up in Switzerland, England and America. Now he was all American, and both of his parents were dead. They had died during the war. Natural deaths. And his brother and sister—both more than a decade older than he—lived in Europe. He hadn't seen them since the funeral. They didn't like him, and he didn't like them. They thought they should have gotten more out of the estate, that their father had been partial to Ernest because he was the baby. But the whole thing was ironical. All right, so he got ten thou as opposed to their five each. What was that? They had both been given better educations than he could give himself on that money and still have anything left. So, being no fool, he'd enlisted at nineteen, put away his loot and had gone to Yale on the GI Bill when he got out. For a while there it looked as if he would one day be a rich man, the way those uranium stocks bloomed. Then they withered and died; he hadn't gotten in on the good ones after all. He wondered now if Betsy would ever have married him if she had known he wasn't going to make it....

The Jeep was pulling onto the concrete apron of the service station ahead, and Charlotte waved as she got out of the car. "Go ahead," she said. "Meet me at Bohack's. I have to go to the hardware store, then to make an appointment at the hairdresser's."

"I'll meet you at the hardware store," he replied with some annoyance.

Why would the fool think he'd rather cool his heels in a supermarket instead of a hardware store where at least the merchandise was more diverting? Charlotte really was something of a lightweight in the head. But maybe Hank liked to fuss around food. As a matter of fact, Ernie himself rather enjoyed food shopping. There was nothing particularly non-masculine about that. Why do I keep coming back to this faggot bit about Hank? he wondered. Certainly Hank didn't look like a homosexual, or act like one. Hank was very lean, athletic—a big tall guy. And good-looking, too, in a way. Only that natty little mustache seemed like an affectation. Too small for his face. Looked tacked on. Ernie had thought about a mustache, but decided against it. Especially after he had seen that fuzzy horror that Bill Roche had produced on his upper lip. Joan, smart girl, had made him shave it off....

He'd have to put in an appearance at the Roche's sooner or later. Better later. He still hadn't decided on his approach. All right, so Bill knew. That was one thing. He didn't feel nearly so nonchalant about the situation as he had last night. Liquor false-confidence. Come to think of it, it was rather surprising that Bill had guessed right off like that. Why had he? And discreet though Bill was.... In some concern Ernie recalled Peggy's underwear and scarf lying in secret in his bag. But suppose they weren't lying in secret anymore?

He found a parking space behind the hardware store, and went inside through the back.

"Hi, kiddo," Charlotte surprised him. "Why the worried frown?"

"My eye hurts and I have a headache," he said sullenly.

"I'm sorry," she said abashed.

In a way it was true. Anyway, it was always his stock excuse if one of his babes caught him out. And Charlotte here was determined to catch him out. Pry into l'affaire Peggy. Well, she wasn't going to do it until he was good and ready to let her. He gave her a sudden radiant smile and said, "My, my, judging from what I see you must have gotten mixed up and gone to one of those instant car-wash places instead of the hairdresser."

"You scamp!" she reproved him jokingly. "I *told* you it was just to make an appointment. You think I'd turn up at the Roche's party tonight looking like this?"

"Party? We're having a party?"

"Certainly. Semi-progressive dinner party. Ten people. And thank God Joan got the tough part. I got dessert."

"Just, I hope," he said, unable to pass up the pun.

CHAPTER SEVEN
MRS. GRANNIS

P EGGY WOKE late, found that her hair was the wreck she
expected, and, with a sigh, donned shorts, one of the hand-
made sports shirts Tom had brought her from Jamaica, and a pair
of new sneakers. It wasn't that she was hungover, but she did feel
very shaky and—sneaky, somehow. But why? What did it matter? It had been a most casual, mutually spontaneous thing. She
had no desire to wreck his marriage. Even if such were possible.
Then she remembered how he'd left her: his kiss had been like a
seal upon her lips—good night and final. Her own earlier boldness contrasted with it badly. She felt ashamed. And, moreover,
that seal upon her lips in place of a kiss of—of what? intimacy?
passion? (well, maybe not. He was probably exhausted, but still
the way he had hustled her out of there and up the stairs …) then
fondness, gratitude, or that delicious little-boy sweetness he had
exhibited so powerfully earlier. Anything but that flat imprint,
as if she were an envelope. Well, she was sealed all right. Nobody
would hear about this from her. She would deny everything. But
now, now it was time to brave the company.

They were all in the dining room, all but Ernest, that is, still
leisurely breakfasting. The three children squealed joyously as
she came in.

"Well, at last!" Joan cried, her eyes wide and happy. "How
are you? How did you sleep? I think Kathy and Billy would have

called the mortuary if you'd waited one minute longer." She reached up with both hands as Peggy bent down and they gave each other the ritual friendship kiss.

Then Peggy hugged Kathy, Billy and baby Mike in turn, saying "Hello, you cute things," feeling false, but not really false, since wanting children was something she had simply put off but would eventually get to, like learning Russian. And they loved her.

Alice, the portly Negro cook-maid whose ebony body always seemed steamy in spite of her crisp uniform or the season of the year, brought in hot pancakes for "Miss Peggy." She liked calling her that. It was a sort of secret-society appellation. Had Peggy been a real Southerner, it would have made both of them uncomfortable, but she wasn't; she was second generation Southerner, her family having come from Valdosta, Georgia, on her mother's side, bringing along the money. Then, too, Peggy had gone to Goucher, her mother's alma mater.

Actually Peggy didn't care for pancakes much, but she ate them with a non-dainty show of hunger—mostly to please and encourage the children; Kathy had a fussy appetite. Joan glowed with pleasure, watching this.

Bill excused himself shortly after Peggy sat down, and she and Joan fell to on the usual topics. Having finished with the temperature in town, whether it would be a hot summer, etc., Peggy brought Joan up-to-date on news of Tom. Yes, his plans were still indefinite; the magazine still wanted him to cover some special stories, and it was possible he might be sent to Yugoslavia. Then Joan prattled—about the trouble she was having getting extra help out here this year; about the lousy decorating job they had done on their big Central Park South apartment in town; about Bill's work, how slowly it was going (this summer he was writing a biography of Thomas Eakins, definitive, he hoped), and about how happy Joan was this year with her garden. Curiously enough, no mention was made of *him,* the absent guest, Ernest, and Peggy was determined not to ask.

"Are you going to want lunch later?" Joan wound up.

"Gosh, I don't think so—it's so late," Peggy replied.

"Well, let's drive into town. I've done almost everything for the party tonight, but Alice reminded me I'd forgotten to get butter, of all things, so we'll go to Bohack's and pick some up, and I can look around and see if I've left anything else out." Then Joan beamed at Peggy, reached over and squeezed her arm. "Gosh, honey, it's nice to see you. Seems like three years instead of three weeks."

Joan, who closely resembled the Queen of England and her sister, had in royal quantity the gift or curse of empathy, in addition to a heart far too large and elaborate for the sleeve she wore it on, or so thought Peggy. Consequently, terms primarily used for weather forecasts did excellently as descriptions of Joan's moods and facial expressions: clear and sunny; winds up to ten miles an hour; showers today, clearing tomorrow. This morning, while not radiant, she was at least shining. Joan was very fond of Peggy, as she had been of Peggy's sister, a classmate at Bennington who had been killed in the tragic Boston air crash. Afterwards, Joan felt very close to Peggy.

But for all of her emotional candor, Peggy knew Joan was no simpleton. She had a quick mind and a good one, and her sense of tact was almost flawless. She was the perfect wife for Bill who, despite his success in life and the handsome array of silver spoons he had been born with, so to speak, was inclined toward self-effacing and brooding—a condition all too clear from the expression on his face—though he always sounded cheerful enough. Bill had nearly a first-rate mind, a dry, cynical sense of humor, and an understanding of the ways of the world that was perhaps too broad for his own good. Joan was his leaven.

All in all, the Roches were the happiest couple Peggy knew. But life was tough, even for them.... This reflection drained more of the sparkle from the day, and Peggy felt distinctly troubled, as broody as Bill. She didn't quite know why. She supposed it was a combination of what had happened last night, plus talking about Tom, plus the fact that she would simply have to do something about her hair. Or maybe she could wear it in a pony-tail, unbecoming as that was....

"Well, come on, Peg," Joan roused her, returning to the dining room after having gone in long search for her pocketbook (Joan was inclined to mislay things, and she was a frankly bad housekeeper). "I thought maybe we'd take a drive after we get through in town. Okay?"

Peggy listlessly said that it sounded like fun.

But it wasn't fun, as it turned out, though it was many other things.

While Peggy waited in the station wagon for Joan to run into the supermarket, she thought she saw Ernest's car. But there was no one in it. All the same, her heart leaped up, startled and anxious. Where was he? Surely he couldn't have still been sleeping while they breakfasted. No, the kids would have made a clamor about that. He was gone, that was all.

"Guess who I saw in Bohack's just now," Joan said in her usual bouncy way as she came back to the car.

"Who?" Peggy asked as casually as she could.

"Our errant house guest and Charlotte Adams. Poor Charl was doing some hurry-up shopping for tonight. She's even worse than I am," she ended with a laugh.

"What's with her anyway?" Peggy queried.

"With her? How do you mean?"

"Oh, I don't know much about her—or her husband either."

"I guess they're pretty much the usual. Hank is fond of sailing and things like that, and Charl is vaguely artistic—paints a little and has published one or two short stories. Reads a lot. They know quite a few of the art crowd—go to those parties that Jackson Pollock's widow throws, and are friends of Lutz Sander and de Kooning. Is that what you mean?"

Peggy nodded, but it wasn't what she meant at all. Clearly the Adams were all this and everybody knew they were quite rich, but what Peggy was really interested in was their relationship to Ernest Marvin. "Are they very friendly with your friend Betsy?" she asked reflectively.

Joan shot her a look, which Peggy caught. "Well, that's a hard question to answer," was her reply.

CHAPTER EIGHT

B UT PEGGY was determined to have an answer to her question about Betsy, and to glean all she could from Joan about Ernest without seeming to pry.

"The two couples know each other fairly well, I guess," Joan said hesitatingly. "And of course they're fond of Betsy. Everyone around here is. Betsy has always been terribly popular—with most people."

Peggy made a slight grimace.

"You didn't give her a chance," Joan stated quietly.

Peggy said nothing.

Joan sighed. "Oh, well, you won't have to run into her this time. She won't be back until September. Poor Ernest, he misses her so. That's why we asked him out this weekend. By the way, Bill tells me I was wrong, that you two hit it off splendidly. I'm glad."

Peggy gave an uncomfortable laugh and shrugged. "He's nice enough," she said.

"Yes, isn't he?" Joan said chattily. "If you can take him as he really is. You know, losing that eye in the war—he was a real war hero, believe it or not—must have done something pretty awful to him. He's really so sweet, so shy."

"He does a lot of bragging and name-dropping to compensate," Peggy observed.

"Does he? Well, I guess we're just so used to him, and so fond of him. And when Betsy's around he relaxes more, isn't quite so defensive."

"I take it that's a good marriage?"

"The best. He adores her and adores the children. You should see him with them."

I should indeed, thought Peggy sourly, growing more unhappy by the moment.

"They've been married long?"

"Years and years. Ever since Betsy graduated from Bennington. My God, that *was* years ago!"

Peggy looked at her friend numbly. "Where did they live out here?"

"A beautiful place! Want to drive by?"

"Yes," said Peggy. "I'd like to see it."

"It's in Southampton, really," Joan said. "Her father gave it to her."

"I thought Betsy aspired once to the ballet. Isn't that what you once told me?"

"Yes, of course. That's right. She and Ern did wait for about a year before they married. Betsy could have been quite a star. But she and Ern were so much in love."

Peggy accepted this in silence, and when Joan spoke again it was on another subject, one which Joan had discoursed on many times and which bored Peggy ineffably: the way the old line crowd in Easthampton felt about the artist invasion, how they resented the fact that so many of the art bunch could afford to take the chair car, or even drawing rooms, into town at the close of the weekend. Peggy, as usual, couldn't make out quite which side Joan was on. In a way she belonged to both, for she, unlike Bill, came of Mayflower stock, and though nearly money-less her family had kept up somehow and Joan had summered in the Hamptons as a child.

"Here's Betsy's house," Joan announced, slowing the station wagon.

"Quite a place," Peggy observed.

"Yes, it's very impressive, isn't it? And it's even larger than it looks. About forty rooms, as I remember. And when they lived here all this was part of the grounds—" she gestured to the right where some new ranch-style dwellings were located. "They cut a road through after Betsy sold it."

Now, Peggy felt downright blue, for some reason. It wasn't that she envied Betsy the house; it was something more.

"Since we've come this far, how would you like to drive to St. James? I'll show you where I lived for a year with my first husband."

"I didn't know you ever lived in St. James," Joan said in surprise.

"Well, I didn't know you very well in those days," Peggy said with a smile.

Now she would show Joan something! If she thought Betsy had a house—!

As they drove along, Peggy wondered at her own nerve. She hadn't been back to St. James since the divorce. She didn't even know if his family still owned it. That was what came of reckless young marriages with both families disapproving. Though it had not ended in disgrace, things had been anything but jolly. However, while it had lasted, it had been idyllic. Viewing it now from ten years' time, the dreamlike quality was stronger than ever. Nostalgia overwhelmed her with its essence, sad and sickly sweet as a funeral wreath. She was sorry she had suggested the visit. For the first time in many years, her memory's image of him was as sharply etched as if he waited on the great stone steps in front of his parents' house—as he used to, when she would come back from riding, and he would lift her down—so gently, so lovingly. Who knows? Maybe for all she knew he was standing there this minute, waiting for wife number three, or was it four now, to ride up on Thunder's back—but Thunder would be done for by now....

"Honey, if it makes you unhappy to go back ..." Joan suggested sympathetically.

Peggy shook her head. "No," she denied. "It doesn't," but tears stung her eyes, and she averted her face. If Joan saw that she would inevitably start weeping too. She always did.

"You'll have to show me where to turn off," Joan said.

"I will—if I remember. I haven't been back since it ended."

"Want to talk about it?"

"Why not?" Peggy said. "It's ancient history. I don't care anymore. My love life has been sufficiently rich and rewarding to make up for everything since that childlike romantic marriage."

Joan gave her a warm smile. "I'm glad you're not bitter," she said. "It's so easy to be bitter about those things."

"Not me. Not after I met Tom."

"You're really happy with him, aren't you?"

"Why do you ask that?"

"I wasn't asking so much as just making a statement."

"Well, no," Peggy said musingly. "But don't tell anybody. Tom and I are holding the whole thing in abeyance until he gets back. It's partly why he's still away."

"Oh, darling, I'm so sorry!" Joan exclaimed. "But then I didn't think you were quite yourself even before we left town. And this morning you seemed so restless and sort of keyed up."

"I feel keyed up."

"You haven't met somebody else...."

"Not exactly."

"Well, be careful, Peg. It's so easy to go off the deep end when you're in that frame of mind."

Peggy gave her a sharp look of near hostility. How maddening Joan was today with all her cliches and homely sympathy!

What was behind all this? Had, Bill spoken to her about—about that Marvin creature? "I wouldn't worry if I were you, Joan," she said tersely. "I'm too smart to get involved in anything. If I do decide to play the field—and, mind you, I've decided nothing—it will be for entertainment purposes only."

"I hope you mean that, Peg. I'd hate to see you get hurt. And it's so easy. Most of the men our age are cranks, if they're free, or homosexual, or much married, really, no matter how they play around...."

CHAPTER NINE
MRS. ROCHE

"WHAT A BEAUTIFUL place!" Joan said admiringly with a sigh.

Peggy made no reply. She was still too stunned. The house had been sold, apparently, and turned into an inn. A great sign, black and white and in elaborate good taste, had forewarned of this at the entrance to the grounds, but she hadn't believed it until they drew up into the circular driveway.

"What a pity," Joan commented further. "But all these great old places are going. Too hard to keep up, and not enough staff available to run them. Would you like to go in? We might have a drink or a bite, if they're serving lunch."

Peggy shook her head.

"No. I can see how you feel. I wouldn't want my illusions completely shattered either."

"It isn't that. On second thought, let's do go in. I'm getting hungry. I'll bet even money they've made the library into the dining room. It always sort of looked like a restaurant anyway. Preposterous room. But then the whole house was rather preposterous. And they were preposterous people—very nouveau—and determinedly Edwardian." She gave a short laugh. "My father-in-law even affected a British accent, and he'd never even been there until after the war when he made all that money on the black market."

"They sound terrible—but fascinating."

"They were that," Peggy agreed.

She's upset, poor thing, Joan observed to herself. I do hate to see her sad, I really do. And I'd hate to see her get hurt—

"Well, I was right!" Peggy said in wry triumph as they entered the inn and saw a small neon sign over the door of what had been the library which said "Dining Room."

"So you were. And I already see what you mean about it being perfect as a restaurant. Did his family build this place?"

"They could have," Peggy said with a small laugh. "But fortunately for them some other moneyed vulgarian had saved them the trouble—way back in the '20s."

A headwaiter discreetly approached and showed them to a booth located along one panelled wall.

"The maitre d' even looks like my ex-father-in-law," Peggy whispered to Joan in amusement.

Joan giggled, and they sat down at the table which was set with a snowy damask cloth, much crystal, and what appeared to be real silver. "I'll bet this place costs as much as the Hedges," she whispered to Peggy. "I only came out with ten bucks."

"Don't worry about it," Peggy replied. Then the headwaiter handed each of them a large shiny black menu.

Peggy studied hers rather critically, but Joan knew what she wanted—vichysoisse and a sliced chicken sandwich—so she took the opportunity to study Peggy instead. She couldn't believe it, somehow—what Bill had told her. Not that he was at all sure, but it looked that way. It looked very much that way. Thank God it had been dark when he was talking about it, for Joan had felt the blood rush to her head, and her heart had paused like a frightened animal before it pounded off again. She had even been too upset to question Bill about it closely, had merely murmured, hoping she sounded sleepy. Oh, Ernie ... how *could* you? she thought.

And right in my own house, in the very same bed.... She knew it had been folly on her part to give in to him, but then she had, hadn't she? Not that she didn't love Bill, and would always love Bill.... Oh, Ernest, she thought again miserably.

"I'm going to have something fancy," Peggy was saying. "But just what I can't quite decide."

... But maybe Peggy was the one who instigated the whole thing, being in her disconsolate frame of mind. Maybe it wasn't Ernest's fault at all. It was the gallant thing to do, of course. And even Bill probably would hesitate in turning down a pretty woman. Of course, he was always consistent in swearing to her he was faithful, and she believed him. And until Ernie she had never once dreamed—

"What are you going to eat?" Peggy asked, still frowning slightly as she gazed at the menu.

"What? Oh, soup and a sandwich. I'm not very hungry. I ate trunksful of pancakes."

Peggy flashed her a smile which Joan answered woodenly. She couldn't get her mind off this tremendous anxiety. She just *had* to know. Maybe it was silly of her to be jealous. After all, he was Betsy's husband. But they had been estranged for years as husband and wife—so Ernie said, and Bill had many times reported this, after his talks with Ernie. Then there had been that apartment he had had in town. But that was before she had known him, in the biblical sense....

The waiter came for their orders. Joan gave hers rather absently, then nervously smoked again. She seldom smoked. She stared at Peggy without thinking, then gave her a bright vacuous smile to make up for this.

"Are you worried about the party?" Peggy asked. "I loathe having to feed so many people."

"It isn't that," Joan replied. "Did I tell you that Mike may have to wear a cast on his right foot? It never did straighten out properly, and the doctor said to be on the safe side that it might come to that."

"How awful!" Peggy exclaimed.

"Yes, but I'm glad we noticed it in time. He could have been crippled for life."

Joan's soup arrived and Peggy told her to go ahead, which Joan did, but found it hard work getting it down. She was too upset really to eat. It hadn't been so bad until she'd seen Peggy's face at breakfast. Then that sinking certainty began, and it had gotten progressively worse. She simply *had* to know! There must be some way to worm it out of Peggy, for God knows she couldn't confront Ernie with it. She had some pride left, believe it or not. She would never let him know she even suspected. And if it came out some way or other, he would never know it made the slightest difference to her, that the whole thing had just been a morning's amusement to her.... But she *couldn't*. And besides, hadn't he told her it was serious with him, that he had been in love with her a long, long time ... had wanted her so? Oh, the whole thing was too ridiculous! Bill was so imaginative, and in the circumstances such a suggestion was infectious. What proof did she have, really? None! Just Bill's suspicions and Peggy's face when she came in the dining room—guilty and yet refreshed. Anything could have caused her to look like that. And certainly nothing Peggy had said so far indicated.... No. It was too absurd. Anyway, tonight she would know more. If Peggy and Ernie had been together Joan would know. Suddenly she couldn't wait to get back. Ernie was probably there this minute. He and Bill would be having lunch....

CHAPTER TEN

T HE HOUSE was as empty and peaceful as a house in Pompeii a hundred years after the lava had congealed, and quiet in that lifeless sort of way that summer houses have when no one is home, when everybody is at play. And Joan blinked into the cool darkness of her empty house, feeling foolish now for her haste, her anxiety, as she came in, with Peggy following, vaguely fanning herself. What had all the headlong rush been about anyway? The sexual mischief of a house guest? What was it to her, even if it were true? She sighed and stretched, dropping her canvas and leather pocketbook casually on a chair. "Gosh, I'm sleepy," she said. "It's the heat. Think we have time for a nap?"

"Not I," Peggy replied. "Look at my hair. I'll have to cope with it somehow."

Joan eyed her friend's blonde, now-stringy hair. "I have one of those kooky hairdryers," she volunteered. "The kind that lets you do the ironing and the vacuuming while your head's cooking."

Peggy laughed. "Good God," she said. "TV's everywhere." Then she added with a smirk, "But do I have to vacuum and iron too? Can't I just sit idle, like at the hairdressers like?"

"Oh, you rascal!" Joan exclaimed in a sudden burst of joy, eyes shining. "I've just missed the hell out of you, Peg. Why don't you let us adopt you?"

"I've been spoken for," Peggy answered lightly. "Now show me where this hair thing is and I'll get on with it."

They mounted the stairs together, Joan's arm fondly and loosely around Peggy's waist, as was her way with those she liked, even though the passageway was a little narrow for such a demonstration of affection.

And even while Joan was showing Peggy how to use the hairdryer, laughing lightly over the contraption and Peggy's amusing comments about it, she found herself feeling gloomy and spiritually droop-shouldered again. It was what Peggy had said in response to the adoption bit. I've been spoken for.... Joan wandered off downstairs again, vaguely intending to nap on the living room couch, except perplexity had almost replaced sleepiness now. Why must I be so sensitive? she asked herself scornfully, and wished with genuine longing for the fleeting and surprising mood-reprieve she had stepped into when they first got home, like moving from a vast chessboard square of black onto white, another dimension where the air was clear, reality bright; now she was lost in the black again.

Laconically, knowing that it was for the sake of the gesture itself rather than interest, she picked up a copy of THE ATLANTIC MONTHLY before she flung herself down on the couch. The movement was so heavy and final that it was almost an act of suicide, as if she were throwing herself over a cliff, rather than settling herself for a peaceful housewife's summer afternoon nap. Why am I so depressed? Why am I so sensitive? she kept asking herself. But she knew the real question was: Who has spoken for Peggy—has *he*? Miserably she turned on her side, closing her eyes. Jumping the gun ... what difference can it possibly make to me, a happily married ... why did I ever go to bed with him? Clearly, it wasn't just to please him, as she had justified it to herself, or by way of thanks for the compliment.... No, one did not get so worked up ... so ... yes, jealous ... if there wasn't something terribly strong and tugging.... She pitched back angrily on the couch and stared at the ceiling malevolently, unwanted tears like acid in her eyes. And once again she was overtaken by a great billowing wave of compulsive frenzy. She *had* to know for sure what had gone on between them.

Quickly she got to her feet, tossing the magazine aside as if it were something dead, something she had killed herself, and began striding about, as if bloodthirsty, in search of other victims. Why in hell hadn't she really listened to Bill's whispered report last night? But his mutterings and hesitations had maddened her, as much as the information itself. It had been like the sudden taste of blood-salt in her mouth, and an ocean of fear had pounded at her eardrums like a tidal wave flooding a cave. Even now she could feel it again, pounding her into oblivion, deadening all desires except the desire for deadening. Well, that was too bad. You couldn't wipe out fact just like that, or fancy either.... She paused briefly at the picture window overlooking the front lawn with its carefully tended flowers, its pleasant shade trees. It might as well have been a study in gray for all the satisfaction it presently gave her; the only reassurance that the vista offered was that it was still empty of all human life. Joan was alone and free to explore.

She ventured down the hall in the direction of his room. After all, it was her house, and she had a right to look in her own guest room, didn't she? It was a hostess' duty to make sure that all was in order, that he was comfortable, had everything that he wanted....

She gave a wry smile at this thought—she and Bill had certainly not stinted in *that* department—and felt herself taking even more proprietary courage from it, as if irony indeed had lent an armature of strong metal to her purpose. She touched the doorjamb with her hand and realized that she was slightly trembling. It was a rather audacious thing to do ... and what was she looking for? What sign or symbol? She knew Ernie was far too precise to leave an unmade bed, and even if he had…. She shook her head against the squalid, indelicate thought of inspection. So she just stood there, gazing at the immaculate, though clearly habitated room, wondering so deeply, so hard whatever on earth she was looking for and where to find it that she didn't hear him. He touched her lightly on the shoulder. She shuddered violently.

"Sweetie," he said, tenderly, turning her around. "I didn't mean to frighten you. Were you looking for me?"

"Yes, I—I thought you might be having a nap," she faltered, knowing that tears had filled her eyes again, as they always did over the least emotional surprise, and she looked down as she added, "We just got back a few minutes ago."

He patted her arm, touched her lips lightly with his own, either blind to her tears or choosing to ignore them, and whispered, "Darling."

"No, no!" she said more frantically than the occasion demanded and broke away from him even though he was by no means restraining her and took off down the hall, leaving him to stare after her.

In another few years, he thought, that bottom of hers will be as wide as a loveseat. Then he turned to stare coldly, appraisingly at the room itself, wondering if he had arrived in time to keep her meddling hands from exploring his suitcase with its tell-tale souvenirs.

CHAPTER ELEVEN

T HE SUITCASE had not been touched. Satisfied of this fact after a swift, skilled glance at its contents, he lowered the lid and, with deft precision, clicked the shiny brass locks closed again. One equally penetrating however quick glance around the room told him that she had touched nothing; in fact, she probably hadn't gone past the doorsill. Still ... the nosy bitch had a nerve. She was behaving like a middleaged landlady in a rooming house, full of suspicions and frustrations. Let her calm down; she'd get her chance....

He started out of the room again, then turned back on impulse. He really ought to do something about Mrs. Grannis' "smalls"; he didn't want her in here snooping about his bedroom, too. Or she might even take it as an excuse to pay him a nocturnal visit—for the purpose of getting laid, of course. And he'd have to think about that. There was such a thing as having too many things going at once—Mrs. Grannis, Charlotte, and now Joan making a nuisance of herself. What a party it was going to be tonight with all those women milling around with their hot asking eyes! Yet he grinned to himself anyway at the prospect before him: not exactly unpleasant, however tricky.

He glanced at his watch; rather later than he had thought. The party was to begin around six, starting with drinks at the what's-their name's who had taken Theo's house for the summer, then on to Connie's and Al's for the first course, according to the itinerary Bill had given him. Plenty of movement, but movement could be darting in and out of dangerous situations all night, being on the run, as well as being playfully elusive. He decided he had better know what he was going to juggle, and be sure of his partners, at least. Therefore, without any further consideration, and without the faintest plan for performing his minute act of daring, he removed Peggy Grannis' personal apparel from his suitcase, folded the garments neatly, compactly, and went into the living room.

"Hi, dear," Bill said as he entered, thinking it was Joan. Then Bill turned around in his chair where he sat reading THE ATLANTIC MONTHLY, and said, "Oh, hi. Looking for your shoes? They're over by the door."

"Thanks," Ernie said going directly to the pair of sneakers which he carried to the couch and proceeded to put on. "Think we have time for a game before dinner?" he asked.

"Chess? Gosh, I wish we did. But I don't think so," Bill said. "I guess the girls are upstairs getting ready now. At least I know Peggy is. She came down a little while ago and went right back up."

He and Ernie exchanged brotherly grins, unspoken comment on the fussing ways of women and their elaborate toilettes. "Maybe I'd better get started too," Bill went on with a yawn. "How about you?"

Ernie glanced up at Bill who suddenly wore a look of open curiosity on his face; he was staring at the small bundle of Peggy's things sitting beside Ernie on the couch. "As soon as I give Peggy this junk she left in the car last night," Ernie said casually, and without another word simply ascended the staircase, leaving Bill to look after and wonder, perhaps, at Ernie's boldness.

Ernie was rather pleased at his audacious bald-faced lie; he was further pleased at the ease with which he had announced to his host that he planned to visit a lady's chamber. Poor old Bill, he'd never make it. Never. Even Joan was too much for the likes of him. He'd have to do something about her—and as soon as he had despatched his current mission. Her "No! No!" had been far more presumptively imperative than his quiet little attentiveness had demanded. Of course he had surprised her. But who knew she was to be found hovering over his doorsill like an avenging angel, wearing a dark, lifeless look to match? Lucky accident he had been barefoot after all; that fleeting survey of her back, her dejected stance had told him everything. Without this telling summary—which included an instant knowledge of *her* knowledge of what had transpired and a subsequent heightening of her desires and rights to him—it might have been days, certainly hours, before he got the pitch. So he had reacted as instantly and as perfectly as his instinct of self-protection had dictated: he had made quiet, mild love to her, which, in turn, gave her a right to repulse if not reject him. It had been a sharp piece of gallantry. But it definitely needed a follow-up, just as the Grannis business did. He didn't want to be cornered tonight by any of these babes. Anyway, who knew what new and exciting little bit of fluff might turn up at this ridiculous party?

He came to a stop in front of Peggy's door, which was partially closed, and gave it a light knock.

She at once called, "Come in," in a voice that expected Joan, or one of the children.

When he stood there before her, there was, for the coolest moment, while she looked at him and fastened an earring in place, a look of complete recognition in her eyes, as if the whole love cycle of the previous night had been played back in a swift second by a movie camera. Then the look was gone, even before she turned back to the mirror and said, "Hello, Ernie," and began to comb her bright, newly washed hair.

"Hello," he murmured back, watching her keenly, yet quietly. And he knew then that he had more mind-making-up to do than he had thought; more than returning her belongings was involved.

When she at last turned again, her hair done, in casual search of her string of cultured pearls on top the bedside table, he caught her to him, very lightly, hardly touching her at all, and whispered in her ear, softly as a butterfly, "I liked last night," and pressed her hand. Then he kissed her, applying a slight pressure to her mouth with his sealed lips to underwrite his honesty, then as if that were enough of that, he murmured the closing words: "I did, really."

Peggy broke away from him with a peal of laughter which puzzled and injured him. "How divine!" she said, and noticing that he held her scarf and bra in his hand, she added, "Thanks, sweetie. I was rather wondering if Joan had discovered them," and took the things from him.

But he wasn't ready to give her other hand up yet. He locked it in his own and said, confidingly, as he looked down at her, "I put them away, but Joan knows."

"Knows what?" Peggy inquired, the brittleness and mirth gone from her manner.

He shrugged. "Nothing, I suspect. But everything."

"Oh," said Peggy thoughtfully. "Oh, I see."

"Does it make any difference?"

"Not to me, it doesn't." Then, "But how about you?"

It was his turn for a laugh at *her* absurdity. "How could it? She knows damned well Betsy and I have been estranged for years."

"Oh," said Peggy, looking back at him with very new eyes.

CHAPTER TWELVE

"I SEE YOU delivered your parcel," Bill commented when Ernie came back into the living room.

Ernie found the remark unusual; not Bill's style, and he gave Bill a probing, querulous look, thorough as a Geiger counter, but could detect no rays of sarcasm, no insolence. "Yes," he murmured into the innocent friendly expression Bill wore.

"Did you see Joan wandering around, by any chance?"

"Nope," Ernie said noncommittally, and without further contribution to this seemingly casual exchange, walked down the hall to his own room to dress.

Dressing for Ernest Marvin was a ceremony as rich in its simplicity, as seemingly unhurried, yet swift, as an Oriental ritual. It was also so ordered and practised that he could go through the whole thing—from shower, to shaving, to meticulous tying of the Windsor knot—without squandering a single thought on the process. Indeed he often used the time for special and pressing matters, for plans.

Economically, therefore, he now utilized the time while he showered to think about Bill's interest in his affairs—and Joan's. As he shaved—for the second time that day, a mark of deference to his hostess and their guest—he wondered if he shouldn't give the whole thing up and get back to town. Of course they would think his sudden departure odd, but then most people thought him rather odd anyway. For his old soldiering instincts scented trouble. All the way around. Joan, the silly woman, had taken her own infidelity far more seriously than he had realized; Charlotte Adams was not to be relied upon as an ally or anything else; clearly Bill's resentments and interests were both up, and Ernie valued Bill's friendship—but, more important, he did not like the feeling he had experienced with the Grannis woman. Yes, she had touched him somewhere, and he had felt himself wavering. What was it? Tenderness, that old beguiler, for he wasn't in the least attracted to her; that is to say, he had no wild, passionate urge for her body. And he had both a contempt and an affinity for tenderness; it could turn him, as it had done in the past, into a soppy fool. And he never really knew the source of this miserable river within himself—it could spring up from underground over almost anything. The day he landed in San Francisco, fresh off the boat after having been in the jungle all those months, what had he done as he sat in that posh hotel room in his bush clothes still? He had cried. And why? Because all the noise and city clatter had confused him, and he had cried for hours, like a little boy. I must remember to tell Peggy that story, he thought wryly to himself.

He had just knotted his tie, having worked it down over the blue striped shirt with the starched collar and starched French cuffs which he insisted upon, when he saw in the mirror that the handle of his door was turning. And there stood Joan, in a highly unbecoming orange batiste dress that made her complexion more than sallow, almost another shade of orange, and her huge dark eyes bore signs of recent crying.

"Hello, darling," he said blandly, not even turning, and, picking up his black eye patch, always the last article to be donned, he fitted it deftly over his withered blind eye. He knew she was watching his every move, her look austere, pained, and yet enraptured. And clearly she had a big lump of something to blurt out—an accusation? She had not returned his greeting. Eye patch in place, he set about combing his hair back into place, arranging it so that the elastic holding the patch made no ridge in the back. Apparently absorbed in this task, and arrogantly unashamed of his vanity, he continued as if he had no audience—a condition of being to which he was accustomed, what with the now count-less mornings-after toilettes he had made before watchful female audiences.

At last Joan's impatience goaded her. "You don't even ask me what I'm doing here," she said in a low, unpleasant voice.

"No. Why should I?" he asked.

"Don't you think Bill would be furious?"

"I doubt it," Ernie said with a smile to the mirror, one for himself, which he was smugly willing to share with her.

"You're awful, Ernie," she pronounced dismally.

"I won't doubt it. But why specifically?"

"Bill told me about Peggy's underwear."

Ernie laughed a little; it was rather like a pleasant snarl. "I didn't know women wore scarves for underwear."

"It was more than just a scarf, Ernie. Peggy left her bra in here last night."

Ernie turned and put his hands on her shoulders and looked at her with his great, beautiful yellow-brown eye. "Come on, Joan. This isn't like you. I don't know what Bill thought he saw, but, number one, it isn't any of his business, or any of yours either."

"Oh, isn't it?" she said in loud anger. "This is my house—"

"—And I'm your guest, and Peggy is your friend, and I hope I'm that, too—and more."

"Don't try to sneak out of it, Ernie—don't jolly me up!"

"My sweet, dear Joan. What are you talking about? If old Bill is so bored out here in the nice country air that he has to invent little amorous intrigues I think he needs a rest from the place."

"You're lying. You know Peggy was here last night."

"All right. Maybe she was for a few minutes. So I kissed her a couple of times. And I kissed her in the car, too. But what has that to do with underwear and whatever dirty sordid thing you're trying to imply? Peggy is a sad and very pretty woman—and I'll confess that if I hadn't been in your house—in this room with our bed—I might have helped her out. But I'm not a cad, sweetie. One thing at a time."

"I don't believe it," she muttered.

He shrugged and took his hands from her shoulders in a I-give-up gesture, looking offended.

"Wait a minute," she said, seeing that he was bent on terminating her inquisition. "You mustn't underestimate me, Ernie. I'm not a fool, and I'm not hysterical. And I'm quite mature, thank you. I simply feel that I must know where I stand in all this. I simply won't stand for being made to look—"

He shook her gently, rather lovingly. "Don't say it, darling. If you'll just think about it you'll realize that my paying a modicum of attention to your friend—giving her a reasonable response—is a safeguard for us."

"Do you mean that, Ernie?" she challenged, tears inevitably in her eyes again.

"Just think about it."

"But must you—neck with her?"

"Why not?"

"But the bra—she didn't leave her bra here, did she?"

"Golly, I don't know. I'll look around," he promised teasingly, and they left the room together.

CHAPTER THIRTEEN

A S IT HAPPENED, and even without maneuvering on Ernie's part, Joan was elected to ride over to Sag Harbor in Ernie's car for the drink course which preceded the progressive dinner.

"Happy, darling?" he asked, placing a hand in casual contented intimacy on her knee.

"Ummm," she murmured, tilting her head back against the leather bucket seat, letting the wind from the open top muss her up, if it liked, for she wasn't just happy, she was ecstatic. The evening promised so much. Progressive dinners, childish, provincial and rather old-fashioned as they were, gave one so much leeway; they might have been invented for the furtherance of clandestine affairs. She wondered if Ernie would turn off some place. For, just after he helped her in the car, and had carefully noted in the rearview mirror that the others had their head start he obviously had planned them to have, he had kissed her with unusual ardor. And when finally he had let her go she could not be sure whether hers were the only cheeks that were wet; there had been something so pleading, so desperate, so wonderful in that kiss. What did he want of her? He wanted, she thought, something no woman so far in his life had been able to give him—qualities she wasn't quite sure of, but was emphatically convinced included love, warmth and trust. A lot. She wondered if she could find it in her heart to disloyally drain off Bill's supply of these fundamentals from her store and give them to Ernie. But wasn't Ernie's desperation so great that such an emotional till-tapping would be justified? Wasn't it more like a CARE package she would be giving? For Joan felt that her supply of these maternal, glowing gifts was an unending river. If there was one thing she had, it was a big, generous, understanding heart. And, besides, she wanted to give ... she wanted to so much. As if he read her mind, the pressure of his hand on her knee increased. Then he removed it in order to execute the sharp turn necessary. When the turn was made, he kept both hands on the wheel, and drove silently. But it was a contented, harmonious silence. Joan closed her eyes, sighed, but did so carefully so that he wouldn't notice how much pleasure all of this gave her.

"What are you thinking?" she asked him.

"Oh, about you. Bill. Us. Does he know, do you think, that we've made love to each other?"

She laughed, an untroubled laugh of flawless ease. "No, my dearest, he doesn't," and she added in sly coquettry, "Do you want me to tell him?"

"He may find out—may have to—eventually," he replied soberly.

Joan's heart leapt up joyfully, as if it were a dog responding to a beloved master's voice. Did this mean—? "Oh, my dear!" she said huskily, her hand covering his tightly on the steering wheel. Then they had reached their destination, and he helped her out of the car with that grave impersonality of his, which he could so conveniently switch on and off, as if he were merely a Carey Cadillac chauffeur. She admired him for that, too.

They walked into the house together, his hand just under her elbow, as if it tread air, lightly as a humming bird.

"This looks pretty awful," he confided to her at the doorway.

And even though she didn't have time to agree, she had to admit to herself that maybe it did. Nobody really knew these people anyway—not in town, not out here. He was supposed to be a sculptor, but so far as anyone knew, he had never even had a show. And the house, rented for the summer, was under their redirection of the furniture and the customary *objets,* downright tacky. What kind of a sculptor could he be? And the woman was appalling. Green eyeshadow in the country was as out of place as grass stain in the city. A big oaf of a girl she was too, and complete with peasant costume, yet. A pair of elderly beatniks, probably not from the real Village either, but the Lower East Side which the nowadays kids thought, or pretended, was the Village.

Bill came up, his grin crooked, a sly twinkle in his eye, and handed Joan a drink (Ernie had drifted away in the crowd). "He just told me that Norman Mailer is the greatest living novelist," he told her, gesturing toward their bearded be-sandaled host.

Joan made a face. "Now that Hemingway's dead?"

"Something like that."

"Are all these people invited for food, too?" Joan asked, her eyes widening. Then she frowned in practical concern; that Mexican chicken dish, the main course, even now being stirred and watched over back at her own house, would never serve all these.

"Search me," Bill said with a shrug. "These people seem—to put it lightly—rather unconventional."

They exchanged husband-and-wife looks and smiles over this; they did not, of course, consider themselves in the least conventional.

"I'll have to find out," Joan said. "Where's Charlotte Adams? She's more or less responsible for this whole *mishagas.*"

"Passed out, I'm afraid," Bill said. "She was pretty drunk when we got here—by the way, what took you and Ern so long? Did you get lost? Then our host passed around a joint, and you know Charlotte."

"Thank God I don't," Joan said stiffly. "Not very well."

"Well the joint's jumping, if you'll pardon the pun," her husband told her. "At least it was till the pot ran out. Now they're just swinging along on a wing and a prayer."

Joan's answering smile was tolerant and distrait. Almost unconsciously she had begun to miss Ernie. "I'd better find Charlotte," she murmured, and broke away from her husband and breasted the crowd.

It was simply ferocious. There must have been fifty people in that small room, and even though the front door and the French doors to the garden were open, the smoke stayed inside (as did the guests). A good half of the people Joan had never seen before in her life. Her "pardon me's" as she elbowed her way through seemed to her like a chant, a part of social litany. And it was an ill-assorted, dirtily not just informally dressed lot; what could Charlotte have been thinking of, involving them in a group like this? Joan made up her mind then and there that she would not have these people in her house, social breach or not. And poor Ernie was probably *dying!* He was so sensitive, such a gentleman, so strict about propriety in his own way. Peggy, on the other hand.... And then she reproved herself for being bitchy, murmuring once more to yet another unknown back, "Pardon me....

Momentarily she was stopped by an impasse of bulky gesticulating shoulders of five males, all bearded, all too long-haired for the sake of neatness (their wives or girls probably barbered them at home) deep in argument about art, probably. It was too tiresome, and they didn't seem to hear her polite password, just talked on, loudly as ever. She loathed to touch them, but did, and when the nearest shirt-sleeved beef arm failed to respond, anger and regality summoned forcefulness, and they stared at her in surprise after she had firmly pushed her pathway through; of course they had not known she was there.

"... She's what's his name's wife," she heard one comment to the group. "They collect Soutine and Degas and all that European jazz...."

It made Joan furious. She was more determined than ever to find Charlotte Adams, give her a piece of her mind, and "cut out," or "split," as those smelly types would probably say.

Angrily she stormed one room after another. Everywhere were more and more people—if one could call them that—and when now and again she saw a familiar face, it was a tortured one, pale with tense embarrassment; it was like passing a friend on a corridor leading to hell. And everywhere, like a taunt, a mockery, her identification rose up, a nasty spume from her wake: "Oh, that's Joan Roche, that big collector's wife—they collect Picasso and all those safe-investment cats."

Finally, feeling that the lower depths could be no lower—that she was lost, that never again would she find Ernie, Peggy, Bill, Ben, Lutz, Zog, George, Eleanor, or even herself—she found them, Charlotte and Ernie. They were in the little bedroom, the maid's room, really, at the back of the house, only now it seemed to serve as sort of an untidy nursery, preempted for the night for any stray purpose—the big inflated rubber sea lion gone slightly limp, displaced on the floor, the bed tousled as if sleeping children had been hurriedly removed, and small pajamas and wet bathing suits making wet, disorderly islands on the floor beside the scuffed-up rag rug. Charlotte indeed seemed to be drunk, but at the woozy, coming-out-of-it stage.

She was sitting shoeless, cross-legged on the bed, her skirts wrinkled and up past any mark of decorum, exhibiting her rather heavy, but voluptuous and frankly hirsute thighs. Her long hair was a mess, hanging down in front, and her makeup was extremely weathered and splotched. Ernie sat stiffly at a distance from her. He held her hand, or, more accurately, she appeared to be restraining his.

The whole scene made Joan quite sick. If Ernie hadn't seen her, she would simply have backed away. He got to his feet.

"No, don't get up," Joan said evenly, managing somehow to sound rather goodnatured about it. "I was just looking for you to find out what's next on the agenda."

"You and your big words," Charlotte mouthed at her in a voice that threatened ugliness.

"Are you feeling all right?" Joan inquired solicitously.

"I feel like hell," said Charlotte. "And your little beauty boy here isn't helping. He won't even go find Hank so I can go home."

"Is that what you want to do?" Joan offered helpfully, much relieved. "I'm sure Ernie can find him—Ernie, why don't you and Bill go round up Hank and everybody—and I'll sit here with Charlotte."

"Fuck off, both of you," Charlotte mouthed heavily.

Joan, with a knowing wise look at Ernie indicated that he should go set the wheels of departure in motion, and sat down beside Charlotte, taking one of Charlotte's heavy feverish paws in her own cool hand. Charlotte began to sob. "Go away," she gulped. "Leave me. Both of you phony balonies."

"Where is Peggy?" Joan asked of Ernie, lip-reading fashion.

He shook his head, and she noticed that he looked very worried—not about Peggy, but the whole disconcerting turn of events. He wanted, as did Joan, nothing more than to be out of the whole thing.

Just then Connie and Al, who had obviously just arrived, came in, looking startled, half distressed and half excited, as if willing, with their late start, to get with the spirit of things, if that was the way it was to be. Ernie seemed to take his cue from them and left, apparently to round up the principals.

Joan patted Charlotte's flaccid hand and smiled at them. "Charlie's a bit under the weather, aren't you, Charl?"

"Fuck off," Charl advised again, rather heavily.

"Whew," said Al. "I never heard of a progressive dinner progressing so rapidly."

CHAPTER FOURTEEN

"I T WAS a shambles, all right," was Al's comment as they sat, the seven of them, around the Roche's oversized fieldstone fireplace, which was now dozingly simmering with the remains of the large open fire which they had built earlier, upon returning. Charlotte Adams slept peacefully outside in the car, and the nucleus of the progressive dinner, excepting the sculptor and his wife, sat cozily together, having eaten the chicken dish which Joan had planned for twenty. With the exception of Peggy, all were cozily basking in the close pleasure felt by a rained-out picnic group, having eaten all in sight, as if disarrangement of plans had whetted their appetites. The cold soup course, originally to have been consumed at Connie's and Al's, remained in their ice box unconsumed. The group had come directly here; had, in fact, fled; adroitly eluding all other invited guests.

Peggy, one eye closed so she could more clearly focus through what she had been calling in her mind, "a dark glass darkly," listened to their words, which swelled and ebbed with the same pulsating meaninglessness as the sound of a seashell placed to the ear. She was very, but not noticeably, drunk. Only Ernie knew how drunk she was, and why. On the way back here, scurrying along in his little sports car, as if it were a swiftly fleeing white rat, he hadn't uttered a word to her, and had sat straight upright in disapproval, like a monument to it, even though he must know that in more than just a way it was his fault. How had it happened? Simple.

First of all, she, Peggy, had had every reason to believe that she was to ride over to Sag Harbor for the drink part of party with him. But, instead, when she came downstairs—the last to appear, it was true—Bill began to hurry them up at once, immediately after introducing her to three people—two men and a woman— who immediately disappeared, once they left the house. Peggy, trying to get her bearings, had followed Bill and the other three out of the house, in response to his, "Come on, kids! Let's get the show on the road," only vaguely conscious of the fact that Joan and Ernie had been deep in giggly conversation over by the bar when she had entered the room and that they now lagged behind. Docilely, she had climbed in the car beside Bill. Then that odious party! It had been as if she had inadvertently been catapulted into the subway at rush hour; she had been literally borne away by the crowd. The first face she recognized (if one could call it that) was Charlotte Adams'. And Charlotte had clutched and hung onto her as if she were a strap, had borne her off to a huddle of people in the kitchen, swaying with inebriation as she went, indeed as if they were hurtling through space on a high-speed, jolting train.

In the kitchen Peggy had been invited to "turn on"; she had declined. However, she had accepted the jelly glass full of what proved to be practically pure vodka. Then another, she supposed, and still another. And all the time she had watched with inter- est—and, it still seemed to her, keen, alert interest, not drunk in the least—how the other members of the kitchen group huffed and puffed at their marijuana, Charlotte included. They were all making quite strange remarks, rendered very seriously, as if what they said made profound philosophical sense, as they wheezed the stick back and forth among themselves, their verbalized thoughts broken off rather regularly by a deep, gulping inhala- tion; and during the pause the others waited quietly, thought- fully. Now, Peggy knew, she had simply been getting herself stoned on vodka—being a "drinking square" (they had called her that)—while the others got high in a different—and perhaps better, as they said—fashion. The next thing she had known was that she was upchucking in the john, with Charlotte holding her head.

How she wished she could remember all those important things Charlotte had said! When? Sometime. After Ernie had walked in and she had heard him offering to take over. Then Charlotte had left and Ernie had put his hand on her head and said, "Come on, sweetie," as he leaned her over the toilet bowl, "get rid of it. You'll feel better." Then, when it was all over, when she had done as he'd said, and she had tried to put her arms around him, to thank him, he'd said, in the very coldest voice she had ever heard, "Don't touch me." After that, she remembered crying a lot and looking for him, but instead she had found Charlotte; Charlotte who had told her all those important things. They had sat cross-legged together on some child's bed, and had shared a jelly glassful of very medicinal Scotch. And Charlotte had, as if by wizardry, gotten all at once just impossibly, rolling drunk. Then Ernie had come in, and she, Peggy, had haughtily risen, not saying a word, to leave the room. He hadn't seemed to notice. Instead, he had embraced Charlotte, nuzzling his head against her copious, motherly breasts, murmuring, "Don't do it, sweetie, don't do it." And the next thing Peggy had known was that she was sitting beside Ernie in his car, and they were moving along swiftly, and he wasn't saying a word.

Now, the other eye closed, focusing out the double vision inescapable with both eyes open, she saw Ernie, sitting quietly in a corner, not taking part at all in the seashell roar of talk. He saw her, too, and, she thought, "Now we see eye to eye," and giggled to herself. Very witty. One eye to one eye. But then he looked away. How had she come to find herself in his car, she wondered?

Had he picked her up out of a hedge, or had she planted herself in his car to be transported here? Like the dawn, the first edge of the light of shame illuminated her. She looked down at her empty, ravaged dinner plate, half of the highly seasoned sauce on the floor. What a God-awful mess!

Well, that was that. That was the end of Ernie. He would never look at her again. It was just as well. Too complicated. She shook her head. No respect. She looked up at the group, still actively talking, reliving the "party." They all seemed to have enjoyed it, she realized, in a negative way—all except Ernie, and as he didn't say anything, she couldn't tell.

"I'll never forget the look on old Bill's face when Lee-what's-her-name tried to make him do the lariat twist!" Al was saying exultantly. Then all at once, to Peggy's befuddled surprise, every-one was on foot, bound for the door, saying, "Yeah, let's have another retrogressive dinner sometime." "Yeah, great." "Never mind, Joanie. We didn't leave you any leftovers, did we?" and Peggy staggered to her feet, too.

"Goodnight," she said at the door, her voice small and calm, as if she were just quiet with sleepiness, and she said it six times—first to Al and Connie, then to Hank, then to Joan, who kissed her cheek, then to Bill, and, finally, to Ernie. She turned meekly to go up the stairs when Ernie caught her hand.

"Aren't you staying down?" he whispered.

CHAPTER FIFTEEN

"I sn't she coming up?" Joan inquired in a worried whisper of her husband.

Bill shrugged, but all the same philosophically switched off the hall light when they reached the top of the stairs; should Peggy need it later, she could turn it on from down below. He noticed that Joan's shoulders drooped. "Poor puss," he said gently and massaged the back of her neck: a relaxing endearment he had discovered in the tender youth of their marriage. But she seemed too tired to respond. Joan took her entertaining too seriously, but then, so did he. Neither of them were good party-throwers and were never likely to be, thank God.

"It's funny how differently things can turn out," Joan mused not without bitterness as she unzipped her dress.

"You expect too much," he said, emptying his pockets of change and keys, and placing them carefully to one side of the general dishevelment of the elaborate highboy. He saw her tired face in the heavy ornate mirror above.

"It isn't that," she said dispiritedly with a haze of annoyance in her voice to match her mood. "It wasn't that I expected *too much*. I simply expected that we would have a progressive dinner party, just like when an architect presents plans for a department store, all properly blue-printed, his client can't fail to be a little surprised when he finds an outhouse on the lot—i.e., I expected us to *progress*; from drinks to soup to—"

"I see you've picked up Ernie's 'i.e.' disease," Bill remarked, meaning it humorously.

Consequently, he was completely baffled when Joan turned on him, irate, beautiful and deadly as a swan.

"Did he invent it? Can't I say anything myself? Kiddo, you forget I went to Bennington. B-E-N-N-I-N-G-T-O-N! Get the message? It's not NYU, kiddo, or CCNY!"

"Shhh," he said, thoroughly astonished, but her fury was so real and of such personal intent that he almost felt like shielding himself with his arms.

"Don't you quiet me, you snide bastard!"

"I was thinking of the children and Alice. They sort of like to get their rest."

"Now you begrudge my sleeping late!" she screamed at him. "Why are you such a coward, William Irwin Roche—?" (and she pronounced it "roach")—"Why can't you ever come out in the open and say what you think? I won't beat you, little boy. Mama won't hurt you. Just be *honest* for a change!"

"All right," he said quietly, not looking at her in her embarrassing state; instead he gave minute attention to the pillow he was plumping. "I honestly want to go to bed."

She snarled at him so viciously that the act seemed theatrical, and he giggled a little, childishly, out of excitement, fear—oh, yes, he would readily admit it—and the advantageous junior viewpoint of the senior viewpoint suddenly gone berserk.

And with this Joan smacked him, with such force that the report sounded like the name of the act itself.

He caught her hands in white fury, but the lightning flash died; was unfollowed by thunder. "What's put that burr under your tail?" he asked in harsh irritability.

Then Joan flushed the whole scene out of sight with her usual weapon: tears—for her as efficient and more dependable than modern plumbing. He dutifully held her rather damp hair as she choked and throbbed against his shoulder. "There, there, puss," he soothed her, feeling weary, yet disturbed at not knowing the source of this mysterious fountain of wrath with which he had been thoroughly drenched; but he was too weary to search for it tonight. Nude, now, he put her from him, as tenderly as he would have a grieving dog, succored long enough, and climbed into bed.

He was almost asleep, despite her rumblings and roilings, like a restless sea before a major storm, when he felt her tense and heard her say: "Listen! Is that Peggy sneaking up?"

At her request, he listened. "Mmmm," he murmured.

Then he felt the sheet whip back, a corner lashing him, like a sail in a sudden squall, and he knew she was on her feet, standing beside the bed. Even the room seemed to hold its breath, so intently was she straining to listen. He, too, listened in spite of himself, but he heard nothing further until the sound of her feet groping their way into slippers thudded softly on the thick shag rug. Then, he knew, she was gone.

For a long time, sleepy as he was, he waited for further sounds, noises that would give him a clue to follow (from the comfortable vantage point of bed) down the peculiar labyrinth of his wife's behavior. But no noises came: no voices, angry or otherwise, no sliding silky slipper noises, no clicks of light switches—just nothing. He gave a great yawn and went to sleep.

When he awoke—and it could have been only minutes later—his own crisp, yet casual voice seemed to be saying something aloud; something vital which he had repeated several times. Then he realized the vital thing he was saying was Ernie's name. How vital can you get? he chastised him self rather facetiously, and turned over, unconsciously patting Joan's side of the bed. When it proved to be empty, he sat up at once. "What the hell?" he muttered aloud, and switched on the bedside light. He felt around for his glasses and read the clock: two-bloody-thirty. "What the hell?" he said again, and got out of bed. He hurriedly worked his feet into an old pair of slippers which he had originally bought for Joan and inherited because they were too large. Cursing these, too, because he didn't like them and because his own were, of course, in that clothing compost heap somewhere under the bed, and remembering at the last minute to cover his nudity with a robe, he left the room.

A quick listen at Joan's door told him nothing. He tapped lightly, and the door fell agape at his touch. In the half-light he could see the bed was still unoccupied. What the hell! And where was Joan? What was this fidgety chaperone bit? He'd never known her to take such a scrutinizing interest in the love life of her friends, even with overnight guests.

He went downstairs, creeping along for reasons that eluded him, stealthy as a houseowner stalking a housebreaker. One lamp burned in the living room—at the picture window, wouldn't you know—and he paused, as if trying to divine whether or not this single eye of light indicated a vigil being kept. It was then that he heard distant laughter and saw the fine rind of light at Ernie's door down the hall.

He joined them.

CHAPTER SIXTEEN

"COME IN, old man!" Ernie cried fraternally when Bill opened the door. He waved a glass at him—obviously they had had to resort to red wine—and Bill looked at the three faces, alight with late-hour mirth and companionship, with a frown that was milder than his displeasure. Except for Joan, there was no sign of orgiastic disarray, and Joan, otherwise modestly clad, seemed to have trouble keeping the shoulder of her bathrobe in place. One white triangle of flesh alluringly exposed itself at least twice as he stood there before speaking; but "alluringly" was the wrong word. His wife was slightly drunk and very disgusting; as repellent to him in her dishabille as a madam in a whorehouse bent upon extraction of innocence. "Come on to bed," he said, clipping his words.

"Oh, Tinker—" (short and very private for Tinker Toy) she admonished. "Come on. We're having *funsies*."

This sent Peggy off into a jet of laughter. "Gosh, Joan, you're funny tonight!" she cried.

Ernie was smiling too, and before Bill had a chance to work his sternness to potency, he found himself with a drink in his hand—as if they had expected him and had even thoughtfully laid in an extra glass.

Joan pushed him down on the bed, threw herself on him and began giving him little nipping kisses; not sexy at all, and not entirely playful either. He got the vague feeling that he was being in some way ridiculed. He couldn't tell, when he had wrested the unfamiliar rough-and-tumble figure of his wife away from him, whether Peggy and Ernie were amused or just tolerant. Certainly neither seemed bored, or anxious in one way or another; they seemed perfectly content to have had Joan's company, and equally hospitable to his. So maybe he had been imagining things the night before. Or maybe it had been just one of those things: they had tried and it hadn't worked out, and so, being grown-up easygoing people, were willing to coast in amicability, second gear. But somehow he was not persuaded.

As Joan jabbered along—she, apparently was doing all the talking, and was, admittedly, being unusually witty, though fey, as usual—he had in the back of his mind, even while he smiled and laughed aloud at his wife's antics, that there was something with those two that he had missed. Had their lovemaking been interrupted by Joan? Definitely not. Or maybe they had been all ready to say good night when she had joined them. Not likely. Everything too relaxed. Or maybe, as he had first thought, there hadn't been any. He wished to God he knew. And then he wished to God that he knew why he wished to God that he knew. It was simply none of their business—neither his nor Joan's. What were they all doing here at this crazy hour of the night, cackling away like insane fools? "Come on, puss. Beds and byes for you," he said to her, pulling her hand.

"Oh, Tink," she remonstrated in a really quite fetching pout. But he could see that she was sleepy, that it would be an easy victory. And anyway, she knew she had had her hour. Maybe this minute of limelight would compensate for the party she had felt cheated of. In any case, she left in good spirits. He noticed that Peggy made no move to follow.

Then after he got her steered upstairs, had helped her heavily across the bedroom, she wobbling and shapeless now with sleepiness, he found that he wasn't sleepy at all. However, he got in bed, turned off his light, and lay thinking as Joan slept. What he was concerned with, he realized, was the question of fidelity: what it consisted of, and what, if any, was its value.

Joan had immediately told him, upon learning it from Peggy, that Tom Grannis' prolonged stay in England did indeed have a bearing on their marriage; and he knew well enough—oh, boringly well enough—that Ernie's domestic relations were as mixed-up, as inequitable, and as stalwart in their existing persistent state as those of the government, and that Ernie's efforts to improve same were all lip-service. In truth, Ernie's zeal for keeping complexities were equalled only by his zeal for enmeshments with various poor, unknowing—how could anyone be knowing to such an extent?—babes. Babes abounding. Yes sir, Ernie loved a good seduction the way a patriotic Southerner craved a good lynching. And much the same thing, too. Ernie was about as lusty as a dead rattlesnake, in Bill's mind. Good simile, too. Phallic symbol, deadly if alive, but dead. Ole Peg. He couldn't believe a lighthearted, perceptive—and, yes, lovely—girl like that could see anything but right through a guy like Ernie. Dapper-looking little devil—and, in all fairness, a little *mensch*, too, but like a toy, one built for boys, a toy soldier, something to be treated withstandingly, fondly, if you were a goodhearted guy, understanding of your own problems and therefore of others—but for women? For women, taken seriously, Ernie was sheer suicide.

Bill rolled over. Peggy was too smart for that trap—and not even a real trap, at that. Ernie, as a pitfall, was more a golf hazard. Something you could work your way out of if you got in and admitted it for what it was—and if pride didn't keep you from cheating about not making par. He sighed, yawned, made chewing gestures and decided it was time for sleep.

But he didn't sleep. Instead he lay in a pleasant twilight zone of mental and physical suspension, making all kinds of wise assumptions, piercing insights as if they were a swarm of birds falling before the arrows of informed guess (intellect).

He worked currently with the material at hand: lovely women (Peggy) and infidelity (Peggy-Ernie), and when these many-hued skeins had placed themselves into the rich pattern, he found other threads to weave into the design—taking up once more that basic background color, himself.

Bill had been completely faithful—who but some moist-palmed, nervous ground-slug-of-a-fool counted out-of-town encounters with hookers, or so-called easy women? Never, that is, had he had "an affair," and never before had he ever much wondered why. The reason had seemed self-evident, just as he was sure that Joan's fidelity to him and her marriage had a motivation with unlimited visibility—as wide and aboveground as the Great Plains. Yet never to have been tempted, consciously so, was indeed a rather marvelous thing. There was Peggy, now. How many lunches had they had alone together, at "in" places, fashionably, discreetly illuminated in sable where they could have done anything together unnoticed except, perhaps, conduct nuclear tests? And there was Charlotte Adams, who, by all rights, should have been named Nooky at birth, thus cutting through a lot of unnecessary red tape; and there was the tasty dish of Connie Gehmann; and there was that lone star deserted state, Betsy, glittering away in her frosty stratosphere, who could probably be hauled down to earth with one kind arm and one real word. But had he tried them? No. Would he? No! But why, he asked himself, why the exclamation point? Why so vigorous?

He stirred, slightly uneased. Joan was always calling him a coward. She didn't understand that he was lazy, contented, practical, decent and couth. She didn't even understand that she herself was these things. Suddenly, his expansive, self-indulgent mood narrowed. How closely had he observed his wife's grazing in that field of fancy? He had to confess to himself that he had no idea what went on in that heart of hers that she frequently mistook for her head.

CHAPTER SEVENTEEN

O N THE WHOLE, Ernie had found it an interesting evening, though at times trying, and, in spots, maddeningly dull. He had even been upon the point of exasperation with the Grannis character who had seen fit to get herself so plastered and so determined to wall him up. Yet, he knew, he couldn't blame her entirely; he could have left her in the station wagon where she had been necking with that hipster. But chivalry and a sense of obligation were to him synonymous, and, when her friend had absented himself to go get another jelly glass of liquor (as she had put it, upon rescue, her escort needed more "inhibition solvent") he could have slammed the door in her face. Instead he had more or less dragged her to his own car and had driven her home. And, once there, he had avoided her eye, and would have gladly avoided the fact that they had ever met, had it been possible, for she had literally wolfed down her food. Like all the finishing-school lushes he had ever met, her table manners, when under the weather, would better have been under the table: she had taken her nourishment with all the daintiness and restraint of a wild animal. So, then, why? Why had he, in that last minute good-night caprice, asked her to stay with him? He did not know.

They had undressed with all the amorous langour of a pair of street cleaners getting out of work clothes. And they had caught the train of lovemaking with the same expeditious and methodical enthusiasm. Destination reached, they had arisen, their debarking comments and observations almost exact: both, for instance, had been intensely conscious of the storm that had raged overhead between Joan and Bill, and were either unconscious or stubbornly unadmitting of any storm whatsoever having raged where they lay down below. He had tried to judge, in retrospect, whether she had just been putting it on, this insouciance, trying to match his own, which he had, perhaps ungallantly, made no attmept to hide. But he couldn't judge. She could be many things: unawakened, stubborn-proud, shy, frigid. But who cared? He knew a mistake when he saw one, and Peggy Grannis, bedmate, was no raving success. Better Joan. Far better. He had known it the instant he once again touched that strange body of Peggys: weightless, fluffy, like a biscuit. But who wants to go to bed with a baking product? As he had dressed (his back to her, hers to his, as if they were bookends ordering themselves), he had asked himself just this. If he had been some big brute of a man, infinitely gentle with small kittenish things, or some small giant of a lion tamer, maybe his blood would have sparkled, burned with the touch of hers. But this way it was nothing, nowhere; they were too much alike, but polar worlds apart, each pointed in opposite directions. And at the close of this weekend, tomorrow, he would tip his figurative hat.

Then Joan, damn her, had bustled on the scene. Only not just like that. They had been decently clad, having a nightcap, as wildly abandoned as your maiden aunt, in the living room, when down she had lunged, murder in her tearrimmed eyes, her nostrils flaring like a wild stallion's. Whatever bacchanalia she had planned to raid and halt, he would hesitate to name, but— and he would hand it to her—she righted herself smartly, made a good social adjustment. And all was well until Peggy discreetly excused herself to go to the "little girl's room."

Joan had taken that opportunity—oh, how she had taken it!—but everything had been on his side: appearances—i.e., their total attire, their drinks in plain view, their murmured casual talk even as Snoopy undoubtedly stole down the stairs, prepared to catch them in a silent soulkissing clinch from which they could make a last-minute breakaway. And nothing could have been farther from the case. But, unnerved, the instant Peggy had gone—undoubtedly retiring to the douche bag as neither had taken precautions—Joan had dug in. Journalist fashion—except her who, when, where, what were couched in the future. Ernie found himself promising: 1) that Joan was to be the who—the only who 2) that fall would be when 3) that where would be an apartment he would rent, just for the two of them, not some—or plural—other babe 4) and the what, vaguest of all, was yes, he really loved her; yes, they would have to reexamine the whole thing when they really started living together. When Peggy returned he had felt not just relief, but gratitude. Her casual, offhand and goodhumored manner was like a dandelion puff in contrast to Joan's musky, senseate presence. Peggy was already on the wind, a thing to be carried off with the first faint breeze, as if air-borne by nature and predestination; and there was Joan, squat (it seemed to him), squawlike, squalid, planted; thriving and vivid like the dandelion flower itself and everywhere—everywhere duplicated in cheerful, determined yellow.

Perhaps that was why, when Bill reluctantly joined them and finally drew his precious bane and burden upstairs. Ernest had turned to Peggy, had put his arms around her and had made *love* to her—not sexual uniting, not passion, not need—but love, in the only way he knew it—infinitely slow, dedicated tenderness, and she, surprisingly, had mirrored this, as if they had a shipwrecked-island sense of fundamentals and affinities. And then they had gone to sleep, as refreshed and as tired out as a pair of infant explorers in a new world, after a swim and frolic in diaphanous waters. He, Ernie, couldn't say it was the greatest, or the best, but it deserved special note—and care. It was an unusual relationship, whatever it came to. And he was more glad than ever that at the party he had forestalled Charlotte Adams' ugly reportage of him to this girl-woman; that he had wafted Peggy away from that hipster stud, and, most of all, that Joan's untimely barging-in had been so rightly siphoned into the proper places.

Of course, a few things still bothered him—mostly old bothers: what if Peggy really were a lush? and frigid? Loving and friendly were no substitutes. Passionate and pathetic had not proved a suitable coupling in the girl before; he'd had to scuttle her, and he had loved her too; had been as excited about her as he'd been about Betsy in the beginning. Then there was avid Joan and his extruded mechanical promises. Then there was Charlotte, now serious about pursuing their dalliance, at this late date. Then, of course, there was Betsy ... BETSY. All caps. Betsy and money had the same number of letters. And this didn't begin to take care of offspring ... letters and letters and dollars and dollars more....

CHAPTER EIGHTEEN

"DO YOU MIND, darling?" Ernie asked when Peggy walked into the living room. He was referring to the fact that he had removed his eye patch, and he looked up from the chessboard, where he and Bill had a game going, staring at her confidently with his one good eye, expressive and beautiful, perhaps because it was single, confident because it was as lone as a pine on a hill. Inwardly she cringed; the withered eye, unpatched, was like a corpse. But we must sorrow for and honor our dead, she told herself. Her smile was, she hoped, not brave.

"What are you talking about?" she asked.

"Nothing. Just my nakedness," he said quietly, and the dried-up infinity of his sadness, his grief, subsided to a small bottomless pool of congealess liquid that she knew would stand forever in her memory; if it stagnated—and wouldn't it?—it would remain; but so would that dessicated eye. Better to have a memory blight than what he had … and he had called her "darling," regardless of the earshot it may have been in. That meant something, yes … even brazenness meant something.

Bill came back to the game, returning from whatever private, paternal, domestic or husbandly duty, and the game between Ernie and Bill began again, as intense and sporting as a jousting match. She felt a girl again, a "brave new girl" as she paraphrased later to a seemingly interested friend, back in the grandstand watching her Star come down the field, clutching pennant and chrysanthemum excitedly to her, as if they were surrogate footballs she could will beyond the goal post. Only this star didn't need her. She could sit quietly, proudly—even, an effigy of herself in his honor. He didn't need her at all; he only needed her presence.

Even while she was having these thoughts she wondered if they might not be a bit prophetic: wouldn't the day come when Ernie would make it clear and cold, a wintry fact—as all of his facts were (he had no human warmth, only body warmth)—that she was needed only for her presence? For it was odd to her somehow that she had known him so closely for so many hours now and their communications system still had not passed the primitive stage, like Alexander Graham Bell, say, when he used to yell "Ahoy!" into his telephone and felt enormously gratified if he got so much as the same message back. All she and Ernest Marvin had done was formally, gravely greet each other, as in a minuet. And if the dance were enjoyable—and for some inexplicable reason it certainly was—and they both smiled at each other and laughed a little at the close of the set, did that in any way alter the structure of formality? No, indeed, it did not. Speaking from an intense, close-knit point of view, she had never had such a Spartan fellowship. It struck her as wrong, but curiously enough, unalterable. She had a feeling that she would never know Ernie Marvin any better than she knew him now. Not first-hand anyway.

Oh, there was sure to be a great jammed stream of backlog information, hurled into the torrents by everything and everybody, plus whatever private observations she had made—and would doubtless continue to make—for herself. But it wasn't the same; it wasn't being close to somebody. And she had never loved anybody before to whom she was not really close, and this had nothing to do with the exchange of confidences—old conquests, old failures, childhood, family, environment, hopes, accomplishments; one could tick off all these subjects in grade-school essays or exchanges with a pen pal in South Africa. No, fascinating life-stories were in the public domain, really; there was an elusive infintesimal something else that had to be added to turn the tinsel on the myth into silver, to create that paradox of a love image who is at once man and god, king and peasant. The ingredients Peggy saw, as she sat silently staring at Ernie, the raw material, were all there, but life somehow just was not. Maybe, she mused, he had been hurt too much—physically maimed, such as his eye, and the terrible lurid war scar on his left arm—and per-haps that was why he had *ne touche pas* written all over his body, mind and soul. Well, if that was the way he wanted it, she would let him be. She would take him as she found him, without prob-ing. Though once again she found it remarkable that she could be plummeting (or soaring?) into love with a creature of Mount Olympian austerity. Well, mortals had done it before, even if it hadn't been happening so much lately, and she would be blindly in love with her blind bow boy, if that's the way he wanted it.

"Hey, Dad, that's cool!" Billy exclaimed at a move his father had just determinedly executed. Billy was, of course, preco-cious, and being ten knew chess in a way. Peggy had noticed him before half draped over Bill's chair, intent on the game as she, Peggy, was intent on herself. In her abstraction, this week-end, the children had seemed more than usual mere pleasant pieces of furniture rather than serious human organisms. She felt ashamed of herself—for last night, with Ernie (the second time) she had found herself experiencing the most horrifying craving, strong as the pull of gravity: she wanted to have a baby, his son. Now it inundated her again, and it was all she could do to restrain herself from desperately crying out, reaching for Ernie's cool, calculating chess-occupied hand to save her from the maelstrom.

"Come over here, Billy," she said weakly, to rid herself of her own silliness, and docilely he came.

Somehow, the child's remark, followed by her own, served to break the spell—all spells and all moods, for Ernie yawned, stretched and declared that it was Bill's game.

"About time," Bill said with a laugh. "But stop making me feel like you gave it to me. You knew after the mistake with that second pawn that I had you."

"No such thing," Ernie countered and proceeded to point out any number of ways thereafter that Bill could have lost to him.

"I think I'll go rassle up Joan and some gin and tonics at the same time. Everybody for? Anybody against?"

"I don't want gin and tonic," Billy said, making a face, and the adults laughed on cue.

"Not for me," Ernie said stretching and yawning again. "I think Junior and I'll go for a ride—time for your driving lesson, isn't it, old boy?"

"Don't call me Junior," Billy answered in mock sulkiness to cover up his delight at the prospect and his near heroworship of his father's friend.

Peggy watched the pair go, feeling a stitch of disappointment. But at the door Ernie turned and addressed first Bill and then her. "Mrs. Grannis and I had better get an early start to the city. We'll leave about four." Then her turn came, and he embellished it with a grin that somehow managed to convey tenderness. "If that's all right with you, darling? Tomorrow's an early day for me."

"Oh, fine," Peggy said casually, though she felt like purring.

Out of the corner of her eye she looked to see if Bill had gotten this status-message, this open declaration of property rights, but his look, as he left the room, to fetch the tonic, presumably, was noncommittal. Well, she was glad anyway that it was out in the open, that she and Ernie wouldn't have to spend the rest of their time out here pretending that no personal attachment had developed. Anyway, in her own mind, it had happened so long ago that she had as little memory of it as old tissue of a skin graft.

CHAPTER NINETEEN

WHEN BILL came back he announced that Joan would be down in a few minutes—the baby was fretting—and handed Peggy her drink. And, in the very way he sat down, she knew something was up.

"Joan tells me you drove by your former honeymoon cottage yesterday," he remarked in a thoughtful pedant tone.

"That's right," Peggy replied like an insolent student to her faculty supervisor.

In turn he gave her one of his surgical looks, knowing as he did so that she would meet the knife squarely. He and Peggy had a particular kind of friendship—a rare one for him with a woman—based on what one might call Basic Truth. On another level, it might be called Peggy's True Confessional, as a bitchy male wag of their acquaintance had crassly dubbed it. But it was a good friendship, and a private one, and it had few critics—primarily because it interested no one else, once its fundamental nature was perceived. It was as sexless and upright in moral character as the Primitive Baptist Church. Only Joan failed to understand this. At first she had sniffed and pawed around it jealously, but finding only the whitened bones of platonism—which her pride in her husband's prowess would not let her accept—she had chosen to ignore its existence and only listened vaguely when Bill came home on six or seven occasions a year and announced that he and Peggy had had lunch together. Yet as infrequent as the communions were between Peggy and Bill, they both put deep value on them. And when Bill spoke to her—*really* spoke, and to *her*—Peggy listened.

She knew now that a new electric impulse was on the verge of being sent; even that first night she had had a flash warning of dread that this might happen, but had trusted to precedent: never had Bill, her discreet mentor, asked for any disclosures from her; she had always come to him, out of need and he had listened and been helpful—just as never—no, never—had he made any confidences of a really personal nature to Peggy about his own life and troubles. Was all that now about to be changed, and, worse thought, was it going to end up being a lecture about Ernie? It could go anywhere from here. Bill was very adroit.

Bill was obviously taking this opportunity to study his material. Peggy decided to give him an assist. "Why did you bring up *that* subject?" she asked, referring to his opening statement about her first husband's house.

"I wouldn't have except that it struck me as an odd thing to have done—for you to have done, that is, after all these years."

Peggy sighed and looked off into the distance. "Yes, in a way it was," she agreed. She certainly was not going to admit to him that she had been motivated by jealousy, pure and simple, instead of nostalgia. That would have been tantamount to spilling the whole Ernie tale—and she was by no means over her head as yet in those enchanted waters. (For a while it was a private pool, a lover's bower, meant for frisking and frolicking alone, no swimming lessons needed by well-meaning adults.) But she knew she would have to say something—and quickly—before he misconstrued her unaccountable "nostalgia," or stumbled on the flat vulgar truth that she had been trying to outdo the exhibition of Betsy's house and former affluence in Joan's eyes because she, Peggy, was so fiercely bent upon stalking her game, destroying all enemies in the path.

"Tell me," he said suddenly, "is Tom coming back?"

Peggy laughed aloud, and hoped Bill wouldn't notice that it was in relief. "To me, you mean, or just back? Whichever, it is a good question, and I honestly don't know, Bill. And I don't know if I want to know."

He looked at her rather sadly, grimly. "Watch yourself, kid."

"I know, I know," she said with a sigh and frowned down at her fingernails. "But what can I do?" She gave him a square look; it pierced him, as it always did, with its electric honesty. "And in any event," she went on, "it isn't one of those Chinese puzzles that comes apart, solved in your hand, from examination and geometrical deductions. I don't know what sent him off—he assured me it wasn't 'another woman', as they say—or what has made him discontent, or anything. You see, he really is a great deal like my first husband. I didn't understand him either." She gave a short laugh. "Maybe that's why I married him—" and she added in a small explosion of insight to herself, and maybe that's why I covet Ernie.

"I don't believe that, Peggy," he said flatly. "I think you understand everybody. Everybody you want to."

"Well, then maybe I don't want to understand him," she said with a teasing smile.

"Who don't you want to understand?" Joan asked, coming into the room.

"My Tom," Peggy told her. "I've just been discussing my marital future—if any—with Bill."

"Oh, sweetie!" Joan cried in sympathetic alarm. "Don't say that."

"She's not being negative, dear," Bill put in. "She's just trying to assess matters."

"Why don't you just up and fly over to England and join him?" Joan suggested on enthusiastic impulse.

Peggy shrugged. "I don't know. I guess I would if I really wanted to. But he sort of beat my pride to a pulp before he left— to the point where I can't even drag it along like the proverbial dead rabbit to lay at his feet." She laughed to keep the self-pitying sob from forming in her throat. "He's even deprived me of my natural masochism."

Joan gave her a tender searching look and smoothed her hair, which Bill noticed and commented upon irritably, if indirectly. "The point is, it seems to me, that Peggy here is being very sensible in leaving the question on ice. She's done her thinking about it; she hasn't come up with any lightning-flash answers, so ..." he shrugged as if that were that.

"Yes," Peggy murmured to Joan, as if bestowing a small, but earned gratuity. "It's too soon to get out the widow's weeds or the silver wedding bells. And I expect that when Tom does get back, it will still be too soon."

"But you want him back?" Joan's big eyes seemed to plead.

"She doesn't know, Joan!" Bill told her rather harshly.

"No, sweetie, I don't know," Peggy said.

CHAPTER TWENTY

T HOUGH NO one was aware of it, Ernie had heard all of the conversation about Peggy's marital doldrums since Joan had entered in, and he had frankly eavesdropped, not caring whether or not his presence in the hall by the stairs was detected. When they changed the subject to other matters—Peggy's unfinished, uncontracted for novel to be called THE DEADLINERS, based primarily upon the free-lance writing careers of her very successful brother and her husband, with one or two mild triumphs of her own thrown in—he drifted away toward the kitchen and fell into reluctant conversation with Alice, the cook, whom he despised. Her arrogant up-North cheerfulness drove him mad. How he detested American servants! But she did say something of interest: she inadvertently revealed Mrs. Grannis' total worth.

She was ironing when Ernie walked in. "Want me to fix you something, Mr. Marvin?" she offered pleasantly.

He thanked her and said no, then she went on by herself, apparently under the misapprehension that they were in conversation. "I hope you ain't getting ready to leave just yet 'cause I've still got Miss Peggy's dress to do up."

"Oh?" murmured Ernie with no interest.

"Yes, Miss Peggy, po' child, she can't iron at all. Can't do a thing for herself, seems like. And her Mamie's gone down South for the summer. Don't leave her with nobody to look after her except that part-time woman she got last year from the U.S.E.S.

But Miss Peggy swears by her. Says she cooks good as Mamie. You ever use any of them U.S.E.S. people, Mr. Marvin?"

Mr. Marvin allowed as how he hadn't.

"Well, they're pretty good, Miss Peggy tells me," she jabbered on. But Mr. Marvin had ceased to listen.

Instead he had begun to tabulate. True, in that brief look he had had of Peggy's apartment, he had thought it rather stunningly decorated and apparently roomy, but these days in modern, so-called luxury apartment buildings appearances meant nothing. In fact, about the only way he had found of telling whether or not people had money was whether their "maid" was a cleaning woman once or twice a week, or a genuine sleep-in type. Peggy's seemed to be a sleep-in type, and, moreover, it very much looked as if she were supplemented year round by still another—part-time or not. If she wasn't stinking rich, what did a childless, able-bodied young woman, single for the moment, need with one and a half in help? This construction certainly put a different light on his subject. Maybe she would prove to be the light of his life after all. For, admit it, aside from Betsy, what women did he know who were independently wealthy? With Charlotte and Joan both, it was husband money; with Angeline—his girl of last year, whom he still wistfully missed because he had loved her but could in no way afford her—he, Ernie, had had to put up the money. Angeline had come from poor farm stock in Indiana, or one of those places.

He walked back into the living room.

But all the grown-ups had disappeared, and when Kathy and Billy tried to wheedle him into a game of Old Maid, he pretended that his eye hurt him, that he needed to give it a rest.

While he gave it a rest, he gave his mind a rattling-paced, high-voltage workout. Hank Adams had filled him in some-what on this Tom Grannis character—a sort of ne'er-do-well ex-war correspondent with no wars to cover, now in England on an assignment for PLAYBOY, or one of the erector-set type magazines. Very tall, very handsome. Smart. Blond. Came from good Irish—old, old line—Boston stock, but had been brought up by well-to-do German grandparents in Brooklyn, mother's side. Period. The odor of respectability had not, in Ernie's sensitive nostrils, been accompanied by that delicious acrid scent of greenbacks. And to look at Peggy—plain, pretty Peggy—who would have thought that she oozed money at every pore? But then, perhaps he was being precipitate; the servant picture alone was not enough to establish her credit rating. But, all in all, it was hopeful. At least the money part was promising, but what about the rest? Gloomy.

Say, for instance, that she was extremely rich; wasn't she perhaps too rich for Tom Grannis' blood? If he could willingly cut out on a sure thing like that it indicated that the woman wasn't fit to live with. Most ne'er-do-wells, as Ernie knew rather first-hand, were notorious for their ability to compromise, make do, back down—in that order. Of course, as yet he had no idea what the trouble was. God knows you couldn't tell from Peggy's own ring-around-the-rosie description of the situation; moreover, she genuinely sounded as if she didn't know. However, since she was not wholly stupid, Ernie decided that she did know, but wasn't telling. Smart girl. What business was it of Joan's and Bill's? There were altogether too many people abounding in the linen pile.

There was also the strong possibility, as witness his own experience with her, that the chick simply couldn't keep her face off strange pillows and her husband found this depressing. I'd beat her, thought Ernie, if she did that to me.... But, then again, would he? Why bother? There was no real reason for such concern unless, of course, she should prove stingy in the bargain. He sighed. The matter would require considerable research.

The research hour, he noticed, was not far away, and he was becoming very annoyed and impatient with the others for staying out so long. They had obviously taken Joan's Hillman and had driven off somewhere; the kids didn't know any more than he did, and cared less. They were as vague as Mommie.

As it turned out, they had merely taken a drive in order to show Peggy the place where the Ed Murrow house catastrophe had happened over in West Hampton. It was still the talk of the region, and the three continued to babble about it after they returned.

It made Ernie furious, and he listened in angry silence. So what? All right, a big unexpected rainstorm had come, causing lots of property damage, including this freak of Ed Murrow having sold a completely furnished house one day and the new owner discovering the next that the house had simply slipped out to sea, a total disappearance. He yawned pointedly, delivering the gesture as if it were a spoken line in the script.

"All right, all right," Bill said with a laugh. He had noticed some time ago that Ernie seemed bored and restless. "But if you still lived out here, chum, you wouldn't think it was such a nothing."

"Granted," Ernie said crisply. The scowl had now left his countenance, but its surface was still cold, like the side of a house too long out of the sun.

"Is there still time for a swim?" Joan asked smilingly, trying, Ernie thought, at this tardy date to be a good hostess.

"No," he said at once. He disliked swimming, and, in any case, it was past two. If they trekked off to the beach, it would be hours before they could be rounded up again.

"We want to go, Mommie!" Kathy shrieked.

"All right," she said. "Did you have a nice lunch, and is your tummy all settled?"

"We didn't have any lunch," the child said sheepishly.

"Yes, we did, too! We had a Butterfinger and a Coke," her brother cried.

"My God!" Bill exclaimed and rolled his eyes toward the ceiling.

Joan, looking troubled, went off to find Alice and get to the bottom of this.

"How about you, old man?" Bill asked Ernie.

Ernie shook his head. He didn't mention Alice's vague offer. "I thought you'd be back any minute, so I waited."

"Well, we didn't," Peggy informed him without hesitation.

He looked at her sharply, rather expecting to find an exultant look on her face, but what he found was a mixture of humble sympathy and sweetness. This infuriated him.

"Any time you're ready," he said to her, getting to his feet, "I think we should get going."

"Oh, come on," Bill coaxed mildly, strolling into the eye of Ernie's temper tantrum. But he knew what he was doing; he'd been there before. Besides, he had children of his own.

Ernie's anger snapping like a rubber band, he said, "No. I have a lot of work to do in town. My report is due in the morning, and I imagine Mrs. Grannis may have better ways of spending Sunday evening than snarled up or hours in traffic."

Ernie's arroyo flash temper disturbed her, rather put her off. It was her experience that adults who had no control over their dispositions were not to be trusted—particularly not if they had brains and some wisdom in the bargain; these assets then simply serving to show the powerful ascendancy of the defect. She frowned at him and looked away.

Ernie was immediately and acutely aware of her displeasure. It was as if she had cast him off. At once he began to modify and amend. "Well," he said, "in any case I'd like a drink before we start. Gin and tonic anybody?"

CHAPTER TWENTY-ONE

I T WAS four-thirty before they finally left, and Ernie was in excellent spirits. Peggy was also afraid he was a little drunk; this impression she got from the reckless way he wove in and out of the thin traffic, looking swiftly over his shoulder as he crossed from lane to lane. He was wearing sunglasses, too, and she couldn't help but wish that he wouldn't. Brilliant as that single orb was, faithfully as it did its doubleduty vision, it seemed to her chancy to dim its full power. But she said nothing. She didn't want a low-pressure system to take over again, and, of course, she didn't want to hurt his feelings. He had a right to be so sensitive; not many people had been as marred and battered and had come out not just valiantly, but successfully. She had watched with fascination over the weekend as Ernie, with skill and steady hand had removed a splinter almost too small for her 20-20 eyes to see from Kathy's foot.

She rewound her scarf around her head and, after a look at Ernie's profile, decided he was through with talk for the moment and wanted to pay attention to his driving. So she herself, one arm carelessly propped on the convertible door, stared at her portion of the shifting landscape. Wasn't too pretty out here, she thought, and was glad she had never been tempted to own property this far afield. The property she did own was far afield enough. The old rambling home of her great grandfather down in Georgia; the equally old and more pretentious grandeur of the estate she and her brother had inherited and sold up in Cooperstown (it was now serving as a private school), and her mother's co-op in the city, purchased after her father had died and the house on 63rd Street had been sold. "All we need," her brother used to say, "is a ranch to get rid of." And now he had a ranch, out in Palm Springs, where he lived with his fourth wife.

Peggy was thinking vaguely that she really should write Buddy and tell him that their lawyer was calling her nearly every day, trying to get some action on selling the co-op. Buddy seemed to think that one day he would live in New York permanently again, and would want it.

"Jesus! Look at that!" she heard Ernie exclaim, and looked. He slowed down and they both stared, as did other motorists on both sides of the highway, at the huge smashed trailer truck and the squashed insectlike sports car it had unsuccessfully tried to spare, thus wrecking itself, too. Peggy shuddered, and Ernie put the car into low gear and drove on, both too deeply shocked to make comment.

Peggy wondered if he, too, was thinking how easily that could have been their car, their blood. Life and death. Just like that. How would it be to die with Ernie? It wouldn't be so good, she instantly felt. Somehow she knew, though she couldn't be specific about it or name the reason why, there must be better people to die with than Ernie.

He stirred her from her contemplation by banging his hand angrily against the steering wheel. She looked at him in surprise. He was beside himself with impotent rage. "Nothing makes me angrier than to see a senseless wreck like that. It's utterly insane! It's insane because it was probably nobody's fault, really. Just a little thing could have caused it—like the guy in the MG getting a bug in his eye and swerving at the wrong time—or the truck-driver." He paused and when he spoke again, it was no longer with gritted teeth, though the bitterness was as strong as ever.

"You know why I know there's a God? Because if there weren't some cruel bastard sitting up there with nothing better to do life wouldn't be so full of dirty tricks."

Peggy found this observation extremely rich in character revelation; he'd given her enough material right there to go on for months. She promptly set off with it for her laboratory, but he stopped her. He put his hand on her knee, and smiled at her.

"I'm so glad you're alive," he said softly.

And the love cycle began for her once more.

They talked a lot from then on; he teased her, chided her about being too independent; said she needed a man to give her a good spanking. Then she said she had one, more or less, and told him about Tom. Except for the details about their courtship and early marriage, her conclusions as to its present worth were substantially those he had already overheard her make earlier in the day. Then he told her about Angeline, and the apartment he had shared with her on 49th Street—only now he said it had been on Mitchell Place, a little slip she caught at once. But then she had known he was a liar, a name-dropper, a status seeker. And she suspected, too, that he had no idea who had put the upgraded address of Mitchell Place in his head. She wondered if it would embarrass him if she reminded him now that on Friday when the matter was under discussion she had told him that she had previously lived there. Let it drop, she thought. That was the tolerant humor she was in—and would stay in, she acknowledged to herself with no particular pride, but no regret either. I will be like an elastic band for him, if that's the way he wants it.

"Shall we have supper together tonight?" he asked, holding her hand, when they were near town.

She nodded. "Yes, let's."

"In or out?" he asked.

In or out of what? she wondered. As she had understood it, he no longer had a place in town, and she certainly could not think that he was proposing that they drive out to Montclair. Therefore, only her apartment was left as a possibility for the "in." Rather nervy, she thought, but, then, typically so, after all.

"My cook-of-all-work is down South for the summer," she said, "and the woman who cleans during the week and does some of the cooking is never around on Saturdays or Sundays. I can whip up something for us, though, if you'd rather not go through all that agony of trying to find something open."

"No, no," he said quickly. "But—uh—maybe we ought to leave the car when we get in town and go by cab or footback ..." He looked at her with a grin to see if she had shared his joke. "Does your house have garage space, by any chance?" he went on.

"Gosh, it does, sweetie," she said, "but I'm afraid they don't have any room. It's awfully small, really, and—well, the tenants keep their cars there. Of course, there's our space—" she burst on "—but my car—ours—is sort of permanently installed there ... for the time being. That is, I hate driving. Oh, Ernie," she gave up with a laugh. "I'm not making any sense. But anyway," she put a hand on his arm, "the answer is that there is no garage room in my building."

Her excited incoherence was caused by many things: the implication that his intention was to garage his car permanently with her (since the master was to be upstairs); the sudden realization that she was *not* bird-free, to live with whom she pleased; the unnerving realization that he might possibly be feeling out her financial dimensions, and last, but most pathetic, most telling, most shymaking of all, that he didn't really *know*, that he was socially ignorant in all sorts of matters. Who, but an Ernie—or a stock-type hayseed, or a parvenu, or a "little people"—could fail to know that an apartment-house garage did not operate in the same way as its public counterpart? She wondered if she should tell him—now, before he bluntly asked, or felt her out in that blundering way he took, masking his method with that phoney cultivated speech—that the car she had in virtual cold storage was a Mercedes? Oh, Ernie, poor Ernie!

"Darling," she said. "I love you."

And the responding grip she felt on her hand told her how much this meant to him—but not that he loved her, too.

CHAPTER TWENTY-TWO

PEGGY HAD never slept with anyone except Tom before in their bed, and Ernie sensed this. But the bed itself more than made up for it. It was one of those king-sized affairs, where both parties have their own sleeping room to retire to, after the fun and games, if any. And there had been some this night. He had particularly felt like it; had felt, after admiring the deep towels in plentiful supply in their bathroom, the casual viewing of the signed famous-name lithographs on the wall, flanking in battalions original oils by many of the same people included in the Roche collection, the genuine Louis Quinze commode in the dining area, the heavy silver candelabra and sterling cigarette boxes, the stock of furs in her closet (opened by mistake when hanging up his jacket)—yes, he had felt this woman very dear to him. And he lay on his side, on his side of their connubial couch, wondering how in hell he was going to get out of going through this Joan thing, come fall.

Peggy touched him, and he clutched her fiercely, surprising even himself. But his vigorous response was far from love—for Ernie, at least. And he held her own declaration made earlier, but not as yet repeated, with great suspicion. But whatever it was—for either of them—it was something. Call it serendipity, perhaps—they had lucked into each other, when their individual needs were highest—he was between girlfriends and she needed a lover. But it might not have worked out that way. In fact, she had confided that Joan had said she wouldn't like him. (Why had Joan said a thing like that?) And he, Ernie, had *not* liked her in the beginning, and he wasn't at all sure that he did now. Only she was such a good thing. So, Peggy, his transient mistress, was going to do him very well for a while, with no complications and all pleasures. He felt rather like a fortunate finder of a billfold: the object was in fair condition, had been expensive when new, carried no guilt-making identification cards to twinge the finder's conscience as he spent the money therein; and, besides, he had needed a wallet anyway. When this one ceased to serve his purpose, he could cast it aside with no regrets and get a new one.

And on her part? Not that he had any real interest in her part, but, in all fairness, he was not a bad thing for her either, he told himself. He was presentable, honorable in discharging his obligations (she had become one), and a careful observer of the habits and needs of others when it was up to him to handle things. No, he decided, she would not be cheated, nor would he.

But, of course, this affair with Peggy was not going to be all glass. There were already imperfections in the relationship (she drank badly if not too much), and if she did love him, as she said, that might prove to be a drag. However, the worst flaw was not of her own making, but of his: Joan. She wasn't any tiny little knick on the smooth surface, she was a downright encumbrance; already twenty times more demanding and possessive than any docile little thing like Peggy could ever become. What in hell am I to do with her? he asked himself.

Even as they had been leaving that afternoon, she had snagged him, put him through his catechism again, and he had made all the right answers, reiterated the promises she had extracted, though at that moment they were more wildly impractical than ever. Suppose there were no Peggy, how could he possibly embark on a serious affair with this woman in the fall? He was far too fond of Bill, to begin with, to hurt him that way. And making a permanent thing with Joan was so utterly out of the question that it was senseless to list any reasons against it. Though, he felt certain, given the opportunity, Joan would demand them. Well. Which made the course all the more clear: she simply wouldn't be given the opportunity. He'd take a knife to the thing right now, cut all strings, all tentacles. He absolutely would not see her again alone for however long a period it took her to get the message. All of which was going to be something of a bore: it was annoying to instruct his secretary, and others who sometimes casually answered his phone, that he would take no calls unaccompanied by the name of the caller. And, if he did get a place in town—a retreat for himself and Peggy, just in case the Grannis character might turn up (he would have to remind himself to go into that more thoroughly with Peggy at once)—he'd have to set up a code for Peggy—and, possibly, one or two other babes he still liked to see once in a while—to phone him there. Also, he idly wondered what effect all this would have on Peggy's friendship with Joan. He didn't much care how Joan and her feelings would fare in all this; he had absolutely no respect for her, had never once admitted her to the realm of humanity. Which, of course, was why he had told her he loved her, and why he would never tell Peggy the same thing. He loved neither of them, but in a different way. The magic words were the only key to Joan's lush sexuality, and, he suspected, in the same context to Peggy's they'd have been like a wind hurling the door to in his face. One liked unreality and the other liked reality—up to a point.

However, all that may be…. He yawned, looked at his watch and got up. He still had that report to do.

He had never had any intention of spending the full night.

PART TWO

PART TWO

CHAPTER TWENTY-THREE

L a peau qui chante.... How many times had she murmured these words to herself as she lay beside him in early morning rapture? And she stretched quietly, yawned in cat-like silence and turned to look at him in his sleep, sleeping in his singing skin, *la peau qui chante....*

It sang on as he slept on, and she felt his satin shoulder with its deep rose-bronze tan. Yes, underneath the skin there was teeming life, a whole population of red blood corpuscles, vividly weaving back and forth through the capillaries, like traffic in the midtown tunnel outside. He stirred warmly under her hand, clasped it fiercely in his, then let go again to retreat from the boundaries of consciousness which he had just risen to, back into the field of sleep. She marveled at him as he lay there in his beautiful body with its singing skin; marveled at the skin and his ability to rise to the surface of consciousness, to caress her and return her caresses, like a deep diver coming up merely to see the light, then floating down again to the depths. For he never really woke, yet all night for many nights he had been able to instigate and respond to this blissful somnambulistic lovemaking which excited her to complete wakefulness. This morning, she knew, he would tell her as usual that he had slept deeply and well; he would have no memory of subtle endearments, the secondary, laconic, but reassuring consensual acts of passion. To him, sleeping in such a fashion with a lover was second nature, as if he were a kitten entwined in the arms of his twin. Again, and lovingly, wonderingly, she stroked his silken, singing hide. Yes, he was like an animal, a gentle, irresistible one, marvelous to look upon, comforting, yet exciting, to hold.

For fear that the electricity of her own arousal might be communicated—her own thoughts darting like bright arrows through her stimulated mind—she withdrew her hand and lay back in his bed beside him, stretched once more, her fingertips touching the Venetian blinds, and saw that she could see through the slanted edges to the early morning sky outside. As she looked, she saw that she could see more than the sky. The new apartment house across the street, almost completed, was inverted in her vision as if she lay at the bottom of a sea. A sea of contentment. How long would she be able to stay under, she wondered, and was he there at the bottom with her, locked happily in her arms, or was she really alone, her imagination generating the magic she thought mutual?

How long had she been under? Oh, ecstatically, she had kept track of the days, polishing the glittering cherished moments of them as they had gone along; each a separate, beautiful prism on the huge magnificence of events; a crystal chandelier of days. They were now into their fourth month together, and had slept in each others arms a hundred nights. She had long since stopped trying to give a name to their attachment. Who knew what it was, and who, really, cared? It was enough that it functioned on a physical level—functioned in actual *real* reality—and if her own riches and daydream powers swathed it in this shining raiment, when maybe it was just that simple thing called the biological urge and/ or mutual sexual need—what did it matter? Daydreaming, too, is a form of reality, and, she felt, she had learned how to handle the crystal prisms so that they could never shatter unless she herself cast them down.

Yes, daydreaming was a good and pleasant thing; not harmful as a drug when used in moderate doses; when the user is aware of potentials. And I am not an addict, thought Peggy as she turned on her side.

It was nearly time now for him to awake. She propped herself up on one elbow, as if her body were a tent and her arm a tent-pole, and smiled softly into his sleeping face, the face of her lover, Ernie; protagonist of her current passion play. With a sigh of faint satisfaction at what she saw, a sigh of untroubled acceptance, she fell back once more and let her eyes again move upward through the angled bars of the blind, searching the later summer-early autumn sky, not in reconnaissance, but blandly, as if her thoughts and her vision were on an aimless, leisurely drive. The sky was as serene as she: of a proper pastel shade, vaguely blurred, as in a romantic watercolor. It's so *right*, she commented additively to herself. It was right because it was wrong and nobody cared. Her love affair with him was like a circumscribed city garden, surrounded by walls: the verdure lush within, and, because it was walled, unable to spread and grow wild. What did she want of him anyway—a home, a husband, a family? No. A spiritual hearth at best (was that true? from Ernie, of all people? But yes, it was true. He was gentle yet strong, kind yet forceful. He was the perfect home away from home). He, on the other hand (which, paradoxically, was the same hand), had nothing he could freely offer except the same things she expected and desired: tender superficialities, satisfying to the heart and body, leaving matters of the soul to realms where they belonged.

How grateful I am to him! she thought. Ernie had taught her what it was to encounter the Compleat Lover. From him she was learning all the little intricacies of this stately, formal dance with its endless shadings and meanings all, in the end, signifying nothing: art for art's sake. For there could be no thought of genuine union, no mutual life with its endless escalators going both ways, no wear and tear on the whole filmy relationship. And she was as grateful for the restrictions as she was to him for pointing them out. In real life he was a married man, as she was a married woman; a father, as one day she now firmly knew she would be a mother. And he was bitterly out of love with his wife, disgusted by her (just as removed in a sense as was still-absent Tom, now more a racial memory than a husband). But Ernie's disgust was somehow different from her own marital indifference: it meant he was totally committed to Betsy, for one does not leave hatred and resentment easily either; the glue is as binding, as thick, as it is in its opposite course, and, besides, Ernie was, of course, a snob.

If Betsy had come from a happy middle-class family, the lunar pull would have been less strong, but she was something out of a Western Marquand, or a WAPSHOTT CHRONICLES of Aspen, Colorado, at least, and he couldn't resist being captured and staying that way by the tie that binds. Peggy knew he would never divorce the woman, not even to better himself, as long as the children were small; or even after they reached full, precocious maturity, wealth and suecessful marriage; not even if they lovingly gave him the go-ahead, while emptying upon the parental head a cornucopia of gratitude and admiration (most unlikely).

She turned again to look at him, this sleeping child, boy, man, and thought: suppose I get bored first? He has taught me how; he has shown me the full instrument board, and I have learned how to operate detachment by watching him do so. The lessons filled her with great courage. Never again would she fear to move on her own, nor would she, in future, hesitate to explore the unknown of aloneness, or timidly wait until a likely co-pilot came by. There will never be another Ernie, she thought, Ernie of the *peau qui chante,* but others there would be....

She turned on her side again, touched him, and murmured, "Darling, it's seven-thirty...."

CHAPTER TWENTY-FOUR

H E STIRRED, smiled at her, running his hand intimately up and down her arm. "Good morning, duckie," he said lightly, in affection, and jumped out of bed.

He went directly to the kitchen of his apartment to prepare their usual breakfast-in-bed breakfast: grapefruit juice, a sweet roll each, coffee black with sugar. She could hear him humming off-key, just as he did every morning, his private praise to God for his happy comfort in this infatuation.

Artificial as their relationship was, they had performed a miracle of winning for themselves. Just what their victory was, even if it was an echoing chamber, or a total vacuum—if and when its smooth sides should become pierced—or filled with poison gases, the perhaps hollow shell had an exterior as pretty and pastoral as an Easter egg. Again she sighed and relaxed, listening to the amiability of her quasimate stirring around in his kitchen. They were as contenting as the fire she sought upon the hearth. She closed her eyes, the better to let the feeling of well-being wash over her, cleanse her, soothe her.... Where so much dirty water had gone before. Never again. He had taught her how to purify herself.

Then there he was. He set up the small tray on the table by the bed, climbed in, and they lay beside each other, arms interlaced, slightly awkward as it was, and munched their rolls, making childlike sounds of pleasure over their food and each other.

"Well, time to get up," he said and immediately acted upon his own reminder.

Peggy watched him rise once more, go through his morning dressing ritual. If differed in no way from one day to the other, just as their conversational phrases, their eating, their kissing were all regular observances. She lay there, her eyes following him as he went down the hall to the bathroom; she listened to the quick hiss of the shower, then knew exactly how long it would be before he returned from shaving, and at what precise moment he would select a shirt from the drawer, transfer his cufflinks from the bureau to the shirt cuffs, would don undershirt (shorts had gone on first thing), then socks, shoes, shirt, pants, tie, eye patch, comb, jacket. Then, "Well, have a good day, darling. Sure all we need is coffee?" Or: "What time is this cocktail thing with those people?" Or: "Sweetie, you know I have to go to Chicago on Tuesday for three days," or: "I hope you won't be disappointed about the theater on Friday, but I absolutely promised the kids I'd come out for the whole weekend." Thus it went. Then she would get her tiny nip of a good-bye kiss and he would be off. As soon as he left, she usually got on the telephone and called the answering service, for one day Tom was sure to come back into her life. That attended to, she then took up her own part of the ritual.

This was as pre-ordained as his: while she drew her bath, she gathered up the breakfast things and carried them to the small kitchen where she quickly washed them in soapy scalding water and placed them in the drainer to dry. Then she tidied, sponged out all the ashtrays, the marble-topped coffee table in the living room, removing the rings from it where they had placed the nightcap glasses; put away the sugar bowl, the tray, then proceeded to the bath. After that, she carefully dressed in the clothes removed and folded on a chair the night before, made the bed, closed the window, picked up her gloves and purse and was gone.

Each morning, stepping into the clean whistling air outside, dazzling with sunshine, she couldn't believe the miracle of it—any of it—from the arising at that outrageously early hour, to the little drawing-room set of polite manners and pat love-nest behavior they had established, to the delicious unreality all of it became a block later, five blocks from home. Then she closed it in her mind and forgot about it.

All the proof that she had in the rest of the day of the existence of this love castle was a key; Ernie had insisted upon giving it to her. He was afraid, he said, that one day she might find herself locked out when she was putting out the garbage pail in the hall. But she seldom used it. When she joined him there in the evenings, as she frequently did, instead of having him go to the inconvenience of picking her up, she always rang the bell. She wondered if he enjoyed the tenuousness, the fine, silk ribbon so lightly joining them, as much as she did. Once or twice he had indicated that there was drawer space and closet space for whatever apparel she cared to leave, but she had merely thanked him. And, since he had rented the place in mid-August and she had helped him move in and settle his few things among the really quite acceptable furnishings supplied, he had said "ours" or "we," as in, "Do we need coffee?" And Peggy took a vast satisfaction in all this, was infinitely touched—and much affected, too, by his obvious need of matehood and sharing. But she was by no means convinced. Ergo, no possessions about his place, no casual visitations at any time, using her own passkey. And she assumed he understood it and the reasons why.

But he obviously didn't, for this very morning, after the tie was in place, the collar adjusted, he said, turning to her, as he adjusted his eye patch: "Does Bill know we are living together?"

Peggy gazed at him, too astonished to reply. Living together? Was *that* what they were doing? How could it be? She had a perfectly good home of her own—far more comfortable—where she conducted her real life, but one could hardly say, "No, darling, because this is just a dream." Instead she answered falteringly, "No, I don't think so. Why do you ask?"

"Oh, I lunched with him the other day. He was very mysterious. Didn't even mention your name."

Peggy didn't find this so out of the usual. "I don't really see a lot of Bill," she said. "However good friends we may be, I really don't see him often."

"Oh," said Ernie.

He wanted to ask about Joan, but he knew the answer to that. From all sides. According to Peggy, Joan seemed to be awfully busy these days—something about Mike, the baby, having trouble with his feet or ankles; then Joan's mother had been sick, and she had been staying out in South Orange a good deal with her. As Ernie only too well knew. Betsy said Joan was underfoot at least twice a week—and for all day. A fine way to nurse a sick mother in another town. As for Joan and himself, well.... He sighed at his image in the mirror as he smoothed down his hair. Pity in a way. She had been a nice piece, but you can't have everything. And, in the beginning with Peggy, he hadn't even tried. Of course it had been easier then.

He straightened, smiled at nude Peggy, smiling back at him from under the covers. He caught her hand, wagged it back and forth, stooped to administer the fraction of a kiss, her morning allotment. "I'll be back at the end of the week, sweetie," he said. "I'll ring you then and find out if you're free."

Then he left, the hall door slamming vault-heavy behind him, locking her inside this peculiar dream until she made her exit in approximately an hour and a half. If I'm free indeed! she thought. After all this time ... especially if the fool thinks we're living together.... Why does he persist in going through the formality of date-making? But she knew the answer: he wanted to be certain that *he* would remain free. This pretext of freedom on her part was all so much rot. Dry-rot, she thought unhappily, and wondered if this state of suspension was really worth it, after all.

CHAPTER TWENTY-FIVE

"WELL, TELL her I called, will you?" Joan said sourly to Peggy's answering service and slammed the receiver down. In her bathrobe still, red-eyed and filled with early morning anger, she stalked out to the kitchen. The nurse was fixing Mike's bottle and Alice was trying to get Kathy to finish her Cheerios: she'd be late to school again, the tenth time already, and school had hardly been started a month.

"Leave her alone," Joan said irritably. "It's her life and if she wants to make a wreck of it, let her." Then pouring herself a cup of coffee, she went back through the living room, down the hall, and back to her own bed.

Should she try Ernie again? Too early. If she could only find out his apartment telephone number. But then she had just found out about the apartment itself last week from Betsy. "Business-reasons" indeed! She knew what sort of business Ernie transacted in his apartments in town. Oh, what a clever fiend that son-of-a-bitch was! Telling her that he could only see her for lunch these days as he'd gone back to Betsy. Why hadn't she known better? Why in hell hadn't she? Because she hadn't wanted to, that was why.

But be fair, she told herself. Hadn't he seemed miserable, that day in July—sometime after the Fourth, which he had spent out on the island with them, without any Peggy around this time. And, oh, that delicious afternoon when they had gone off to Montauk by themselves! Yes, that day at lunch in that little

Armenian place, he had seemed so unhappy, so hot, so tired, so stuffed up with a summer cold, his lovely eye watering—and he had said, "I'm afraid I have some bad news, darling."

"Bad news for us, Ernie?"

And he had squeezed her hand, long and passionately. "You know I have to make that trip to the Coast—"

"Yes," she had said with a nod, "but you don't leave until the first—"

"That's just it," he had said. "I have to go to Colorado in the morning. I'll be there for two weeks with the kids, and then I'll leave for the Coast from there."

"When will you be back?" she remembered now the terrible degree of her own forlorness.

Again the squeeze to her white-gloved hand. "Darling, I'm afraid I'll be away at least a month. Then, when Betsy and the kids get back...." He trailed off the sentence, giving her a look of deep longing and regret.

"It just isn't going to work for us, is it, Ernie?" she had sobbed and—oh, shamefully—applied a Kleenex to her frankly flowing eyes.

He had shaken his head sorrowfully. "No, duckie. I'm afraid not. Betsy's laid down the law—and even if she hadn't, I'm terribly worried about the kids. That's why I'm stopping off in Colorado, just to be with them. Betsy, in her usual irresponsible fashion, has decided to take a motor trip to Mexico with some of her friends."

I hope she kills herself, Joan found herself thinking meanly. She continued to weep, more or less silently throughout their lunch.

"Don't," he had said once or twice, but barely able to mouth the words without bursting into open grief, she had murmured, "I just can't help it."

After he left her, putting her into a cab on the corner of Lex and 26th Street, she had gulped and cried all the way up to Gracie Terrace.

Well, that's that, she had thought to herself as she unabashedly paid the driver, overtipping him to compensate for the use she had made of his taxi. But it had been by no means that. Ernie remained in her thoughts week after week.

To be sure, she did not trust him, and she carefully checked, so she had thought, to see if he really had gone to Colorado. First, she had telephoned his office the very next day, and, when his secretary's bright voice came back, "Just a moment and I'll see if he's in," Joan had gone into a black tailspin of panic and rage. If he had really gone, wouldn't his secretary have been the first to know? "I'm sorry," the woman had said, returning. "I thought I could catch him, but he's gone. Is there any message? I expect he'll be phoning in."

No. No message.

But just to make sure, she had put Bill up to phoning him, on the pretext that she was too busy, to ask him up for drinks. Bill had been given the same glib brush-off—if it was that. Even now, Joan did not know to what extent Ernie had been lying. But she knew this: not since that Fourth of July weekend, had she really been alone with him—unless one wanted to count those noisy, wildly unsatisfactory lunches they had shared in crowded places, scattered sparsely over the last few months. Thank God for Mother's heart attack, she told herself now, weeping once more into the soggy Kleenex. If she hadn't had occasion to visit South Orange so often, and hence to drop in on Betsy.... How, she wondered, had Betsy come to tell her about Ernie's New York apartment? She wished she could remember *all* the circumstances ... but Betsy was always so close-mouthed these days about Ernie and his comings and goings, and, of course, she, Joan, simply could not afford to be particularly interested....

Minutely, she swept back hysterically through her recollections—what she had seen and heard of him in the last few months. Just after Labor Day there had been that dreadful cocktail party which he and Betsy had given out there. He had tried to corner her then—or had it been the other way around?—only Bill had seemed particularly watchful, for some reason. Oh, she couldn't even be sure what was the reason now. And how terribly long it had been since he had been free to lunch with her! She had been in a jealous agony the other day when Bill, her own husband, calmly announced he had lunched with Ernie himself. And why was it he never called her any more? Even Peggy said she saw him occasionally. Why must he be so circumspect with her? It couldn't be that he was tired of her—they had never even gotten started.

That, she told herself, might be it. Out of sight with a man like that was so much out of mind. But who was this new person for whom he had rented an apartment? The one thing she had not learned from Betsy was when Ernie had rented it. It couldn't have been so long ago, Joan reasoned, or somehow she would have known of it before. Say, a week or so, a month at the most. And hadn't he been out of town a lot again? At least that was the message she got when she called him at the office. When had she phoned last? Oh, she couldn't remember. Why couldn't she remember? What a trusting ass I am she thought.

She transferred herself from her rumpled bed to the equally rumpled and cluttered chaise longue, where the long-cord telephone seemed to be situated at the moment. It rewarded her by ringing.

"You called," said Peggy's pleasant easy voice.

"Yes, sweetie, I did," Joan said, adjusting hers to match the soft calm of her friend's. "What on earth were you doing out at that ungodly hour this morning?"

Peggy's gentle laugh came back. "I wasn't out," she said. "I've just gotten smart in my old age. Why have an answering service if you don't use them?"

"But you're the one who says you can't stand to hear a telephone ringing—"

"I can't ordinarily," Joan heard Peggy sigh. "But so many things these days, sweetie...."

"Meaning Tom?"

"Yes, mostly Tom, I suppose," Peggy's voice sounded wistful.

"How long's it been now?"

"Oh, I haven't heard from him since August, unless you can count that drunken call from Copenhagen when he swore he was trying to reach the Overseas Press Club here. When did I tell you that was?"

"Oh, maybe ten days ago," Joan supplied idly. She remembered the incident. Poor Peggy. Tom had called Peggy in the middle of the night, so she had said, and it had taken her a full ten minutes to convince him that it was she he was talking to, not some operator. Then he had talked undying-love, soul-baring gibberish for the next half hour. "You have your problems," Joan now sighed commiseratingly into the telephone, but thinking how to cut all this short as she had her own.

"Yes, and can you hear that racket?" Peggy asked, and paused. In the remote distance, Joan could hear the sounds of the pile driver which was tearing down a building ten floors below Peggy's apartment house, on the opposite corner.

"Poor sweetie," murmured Joan, adding a sigh which was really for her own impatience.

"Well," said Peggy, sensing Joan's reluctance to carry on with this vacant conversation, "I just thought I'd return your call."

"Oh, that's right," Joan brightened. "I wondered if you'd like to come for dinner Friday night."

She heard the hesitation, as explicit in Peggy's wordless pause as though it had been voiced. "I have sort of a date."

"Oh, you!" Joan scoffed mildly. "You always have sort of a date these days. Who's the lucky man—or men? Don't give me that Great Books jazz again."

Peggy laughed. "No, it's not one of my 'outside interests,' as Tom calls them. As a matter of fact, if I have a date at all, I won't know until Friday morning. He's out of town."

"Oh?" Joan said hurriedly, now eager to wind this whole thing up. "Well, that's too bad, sweetie—unless of course you want to bring him along. There'll be Connie and Al, and the Adams', I think. They've asked us over so many times I'm ashamed to accept."

For a moment the phone seemed so dead that Joan thought they might have been disconnected.

"I don't know," Peggy's voice came faintly. "I'd like to come, with or without him—but."

"But what?"

Peggy gave a short nervous laugh. "It's all a little awkward. If it were just you and Bill, but with Charlotte and Hank, too...."

"Who is it?" Joan asked instantly. Her throat, even before she heard the dreaded name, felt as if a hand were closing over it, tightening, tightening.

Then Peggy said it. "It's Ernie, Ernie Marvin, Joan. I'm not sure how he'd feel about going out to a dinner party with a lot of Betsy's friends around—"

"How long has this been going on, baby doll?" Joan asked huskily.

CHAPTER TWENTY-SIX

W HEN PEGGY hung up the white and blue telephone in the den (decorated in what that expensive chi-chi silly queen had called "water blue, to match your eyes," and even at the time she had thought he was being bitchy, and had coldly told him her eyes didn't happen to be watery) she knew she had made a dire tactical mistake. What had made her tell Joan about Ernie, after all these months? But had she told her anything she hadn't told her already? Apparently, to judge from Joan's change of tone. From the moment Peggy had indicated that it was someone Joan and the Adams and the Gehmanns knew in common, she sensed something, and something she didn't like. Joan's voice had dropped down two registers, like a church organ with frozen pipes. She had positively wheezed. But Peggy from then on had told her absolutely *rien,* though she could do nothing to wrest that suspiciousness and quality of distaste from Joan's tone. And the insinuations ... ! But Peggy had told her nothing. Now, she wondered, where would Joan take it from there? She'd rush immediately to Bill, of course. But the beautiful part of the whole thing, she could not help reassuring herself with an inward smile, was that she and Ernie had confided in no one. They had been veritable paragons of discreet behavior. Once or twice, it was true, they had met acquaintances in Fanny's, the little *boîte* down the block from his apartment, because they liked to go in for a stinger before going home, and to listen to that amusing Calypso pair who, between them, weighed as much as a thousand pound canary, as the joke went a few years ago. Then, too, Ernie seemed to take a great deal of pleasure in Fanny's gross and obscene sense of humor—lots of four-letter English words mixed in with Yiddish. But lately, since observing, shrewd Fanny had inquired of them in her mannish croak, "Why the hell don't you two get married?" Ernie seemed to have lost his taste for the place. It had amused Peggy very much, especially since it had been she who quickly pointed out, "Oh, but we *are* married— only not to each other."

Had this offended Ernie?

Today she knew only slightly better than she had a hundred less dazzling, less heady days before, what offended him and what did not. All she had learned was to be able to detect when he *was* offended. And now she had the feeling in her bones that he would be offended if he learned of her inadvertent slip about their tentative date on Friday night. Why, she recalled, our date isn't for Friday! "I'll ring you at the end of the week," had been his words. That could be anytime, except Peggy knew her interpretation was far less loose! Yes, admit it; she was hooked. Just this little thing proved it. She was so much in his thrall that any day—from Wednesday onward she would have unconsciously considered the end of the week, and therefore to be kept open for his ring.

A fine state of affairs! Time to retrench, my girl, she told herself sharply. But, she thought, as she paced up and down the small confines of the den, absently gazing from its blue and whiteness to the blue sky beyond her window and the blue light of the East River, I can't do a thing until he gets back. What a blessing he's gone out of town before Joan gets her claws into him. But, suppose, finding him unreachable, she calls Betsy? She wouldn't do a stupid and useless thing like that, not Joan. But how strange and ominous Joan had sounded … so righteous, so angry. Why? All I said was that Ernie was so quiet and strange, but then I added that I didn't know him very well. Why had Joan said, "You'd better thank your lucky stars for that!" What was it about Ernie that Peggy didn't know? Did Betsy suspect something between Peggy and her husband? Ernie had assured her not. "Oh, she knows I keep some babe with me in town now and again," he had said, oh, so long ago. Right at the very beginning. Perhaps it had even been at dinner that first Sunday night they had had Candid Conversation Number One. Or the next night—Peggy didn't know. How the rich pattern of the days and nights, with their intimacies, their growing together, had run into each other! But now she did more or less recall that conversation about Betsy. It had been horrid in a way, but Peggy could not say she was sorry to know. It helped her in understanding him; or in trying to. Actually, nothing he said or overtly did—did according to conscious plan, that is—helped there.

Betsy was years older than he—far older than she looked. He married her, he frankly confessed, because she was not poor and because she was the most fascinating—and one of the most beautiful and poised—women he had ever met. Like Peggy and Ernie, they had gone to bed together immediately, and, not long afterwards, they had married. Very big wedding.

Ernie's version of the courtship and marriage was at curious variance with that Peggy had had from Joan. And Joan, of all people, should know, seeing that Joan and Betsy had been roommates in college. Joan was only a few years older than Peggy herself, so even if Betsy were older than Joan, how senior to Ernie could she be? Also, it was Peggy's recollection that there had been a year's wait before they married and moved out to the Hamptons—that day on the house-touring drive, when she, herself, had done that shymaking bit about showing off the house at St. James....

Nonetheless, Peggy had listened quietly, sombrely to Ernie as he respun the tale of his marital past, both of them believing, for the nonce, every word. Things had never gone really well; while he frankly worshiped Betsy in a way, she was cold sexually, and he wanted children. Finally she had agreed to it, had agreed to give up her dancing career—had Peggy ever seen her? No? She had frequently been compared to Tall-chief—and had had his son. Then, by Cesarian, two and a half years later, his daughter. Then a radical hysterectomy. "You see, she didn't want to go through all that again," he said quietly. "Not any part of it. And she got furious at me one night and said, 'Look, if you're so hot, brother, I'd advise you to get a little something going on the side. All I know is that I want you to stay out of my bed.' "

"How awful!" Peggy had murmured in shocked compassion.

"Well, I did just that," Ernie had told her with his crooked smile—the one he seldom wore except when deeply moved. "But I wasn't what you might call really unfaithful to her—I never actually deserted her. Because I still adored her in a way—and I like her tremendously. I enjoy being with her, just as a person, more than with any woman I've ever known. Then there were my children. Hers, too, of course. They're absolutely brilliant, Peggy. Wonderful children. They have the best of us both. And it's fascinating to watch them grow up, see their minds develop. They're like no children you ever saw. When Diedre was three she was reading as well as the Roche's daughter reads now, at ten, or whatever she is."

"Eight," said Peggy.

"And Paul could read the directions—really understand them, equally as well as I—for his own model airplanes when he was five. They're remarkable. Both of them speak French already, German and—"

"You really love them, don't you?" Peggy said slowly.

He nodded.

"Then why don't you stay with Betsy, at least until they get past the difficult period?"

Here, if anywhere, was the proper place for Ernie to say, if ever he was to say it to her: "Because I've met you." But, instead, he said, "After Angeline I tried. Oh, God, I tried—for the kids' sakes, hers, mine, too, I suppose."

"Yes," Peggy said rather wryly, "Joan told me that you and Betsy were a devoted couple."

"Did she? Well, last year—for seven or eight months, at least—after the thing with Angeline ended, we tried to put up an appearance, even after we both knew the reconciliation was hopeless. But I'm sorry Joan told you that, though I don't think she was trying to hurt you."

"Maybe discourage me?" Peggy asked, wryly again, accompanying the question with a wry smile.

"A possibility," he admitted. "But I think old Joanie just can't stand not to see marriages work—on the surface, at least. She's something of a Pollyanna."

"Is she ever!" Peggy seconded. "A heart of gold. She wants everybody to be as happy as she and Bill are."

Ernie shrugged slightly and looked away, neither agreeing nor disagreeing. "She couldn't stand Angeline, that's a fact," he smiled ruefully to himself.

"Did she know all about Angeline?"

"She thought she did, but actually she didn't. Though perhaps I did let fall a few things that Bill may have repeated—though I doubt it. He doesn't gossip."

"How long did the Angeline thing last?"

"You want the truth?"

"Of course."

"Actually it wasn't over until I met you. You put the finishing touches on it. I saw her for the last time the first week you and I were together...."

CHAPTER TWENTY-SEVEN

NOW, CALCULATING, as she had not that hot day in August when the stars in her eyes had still been overflowing, shooting off into her head, marring her sanity—on that first day they had "lived together"—she came up with a number of things, then unnoticed. His strange three-hour disappearance one night when he had gone out to buy her some bobby pins. And all those midweek "trips" he had had to go on in that period. Undoubtedly he had been seeing Angeline.

And, in those early days, he had spoken to Peggy of Angeline as deprecatingly, if with more gentleness, as he had of his wife Betsy. Angeline was a hopeless lush ("I am a hopeful one," Peggy had quipped humorously, but it had gone over his head through inattention); she couldn't do anything for herself, not even sew on a button; she had been lousy at her jobs—he, Ernie, had had to find one for her—finally in Wheeling, West Virginia—just to get her settled, out of his hair. Why, Angeline, who at thirty had never been married and, of course, begged him to change all this, had even come to think of his children as her own. She was always sending them little anonymous gifts. Pathetic, Peggy had said, and meant it. But appalling, too, which she had not said. If Ernie could not see how revealing all of his vilifying confessions were, well, the best thing to do was tiptoe off, not look back, and keep him as often as possible from turning his head in the direction of his past, which he so obviously distorted for such obvious reasons. She had said she would have him as he was; but "as is" had no business changing after the bargain was struck.

Of course he kept pleasing her with little flatteries and favors which added to his already brimming treasure house of charm—all amassed in her own hidden caverns, reserved for the cast-off, casually dropped gems which those she loved constantly lavished, seemingly dripped with, especially on initial acquaintance. And one of the best of these jewels, so modest, yet so shining, was a solid gold plaque of charming, forthright admission that he had parted, for good, from his true love, Angeline, because of *her*. It was worthy of a special setting, in a diadem designed for it alone.

She had checked out this acquisition many times; had found it to be true. No early morning calls from whiny female voices had bothered their rest. And, aside from the few "out-of-town trips," of a few days' duration taken in the beginning, the rest of the time he had been with her. In late August they had flown to the Coast, he stopping off in Colorado for two days to see his children, and had not returned until after the first. Then, after Betsy came back, bringing the kids, he had spent a number of weekends there in Montclair with them. Understandable. Anyway, it had given Peggy a breather. So, should she begrudge him those first weeks of their relationship when he had lied about being out of town? When he had really been settling poor Angeline?

Poor Angeline, she thought again now, and wondered what she had been like. And to think the poor soul had wept and hoped and abided with him for so long—Peggy was still vague as to the number of years, if there had, indeed, been years. And then, by his own admission, there had been little amusements in between. And, it was true, that there in the beginning of life in "their" apartment he had seemed to get an awful lot of telephone calls along about seven, though he had sworn to her, Peggy, that he had given *nobody* the number (cautioned her not to) and that he never answered the phone. Still, she had also noticed, he answered it a great deal—and without hesitation—when she herself called unexpectedly. Oh, well. Ernie was a rather confused guy. And she had long since ceased to expect to hear the truth pass his lips, except occasionally. His lies were so flawed and heavy, for the most part, that it seemed he told them merely to keep up appearances and yet to remain honest.

Perhaps, she told herself now, it would have been better, Tom or no Tom, if she had insisted upon his moving in with her. Mamie, though she had loathed him the instant she came back from North Carolina in August, would have adjusted to him in time. Might even have come to downright like him, as Louise, the part-time maid did. And together, Louise and Mamie, they could have helped Peggy build her defenses against the day when Tom, knight errant, would return to his ruined castle. But no. They did not please Ernie. And, he said, he equally loathed doormen, elevator men—all incipient CIA spies.

Peggy had then suggested that she move; that they find a place to live together. But he had firmly, perhaps wisely, shaken his head. "I have a wife; you have a husband. Let's not play this thing too fast and thick. You don't know what you're going to do with Tom, and you said yourself that I should stay married—at least in name, and turn up there on weekends—until the children are beyond the stage when it will really hurt them."

Shortly afterwards, through the Sunday paper, he had found a furnished apartment. It was tacitly understood from the beginning—at least by Ernie—that it was *their* apartment. Yet why was it, Peggy asked herself, yet again, she had never felt like moving anything in?

I've been up far too early for too many mornings, she told herself, blotting out a tasteless cigarette, and going to her bathroom for a dexedrine and an aspirin; she had already had a vitamin pill. And, admit it, she had not been too sober the night before. Had Ernie noticed? Probably. Idly she wondered if he had been lying this time. Was he really going out of town? Then she was convinced that he was telling the truth. It had been a long time now since she had caught him in a real lie; a long time since the apartment phone had set up its seven o'clock tune, which he responded to in cryptic endearments, never accompanied by any specific promises for meetings. By all rights, she should be sure of him. But the Joan flare-up had shaken her. Why? And it had made Peggy think—a lot of things she had put from her mind, absorbed as she had been with the near-cloudless, near-perfection of it all. It was true, there were uglinesses—things even now she just didn't care to bring to mind: his vulgar open flirtation with that wild-haired sprite of a Peter Pan at that U.N. cocktail party, and, once or twice, to put his nose back in joint, she had ordered little gee-gaws for him from Cartier's, which had pleased him with the same wide-eyed pleasure a child would have had from a paste replica of a set of the Crown Jewels. But such little concessions to his contentment....

I wonder, she thought, if I should try and catch him before he leaves town today, just to say that Joan has asked me to dinner on Friday; him, too, and explain why.

She dialed his office number; something she hadn't done for weeks.

CHAPTER TWENTY-EIGHT

A T HIS office, the receptionist, who was no mental slouch, said that Mr. Marvin was out, and asked if she could take a message.

"Has he left town, or is he just out?" Peggy pressed, and listened as the woman turned and consulted someone in the background.

"He'll be back around two," the receptionist returned to say.

Peggy thanked her, wishing she had asked for Ernie's secretary who could have given her details, for Peggy desperately wanted Ernie to be out of town, not just out to lunch, because he had said he was going. Don't be a liar now, darling, she whispered telepathically.

Then she phoned Abby, to find out if they were still lunching and shopping later, and looked at her calendar for the rest of the week. It was full of question marks; all because of that bastard, she huffily reminded herself. These days she never accepted invitations outright until she knew what Ernie was going to do. Really, whatever else happened, that had to stop. On the spur of the moment, she called several of the question marks and confirmed the dates, Ernie or no Ernie. Besides, she could bring him along at the last minute to most of the places.

These included a cocktail party given by friends of her late mother, people in their dotage who had continued to drink too much, and, in consequence, had no retention or concern for new names and faces; an art exhibition where she and Ernie might run into a few people they knew in common, but it wouldn't much matter; a dinner party at some friends of Tom's (that was definitely out for Ernie); and a buffet thing on Sunday night in Connecticut; the sort of thing one accepted carte blanche, but didn't attend if the Saturday night hangover or the traffic proved too much.

Now she dressed for her lunch-shopping with her friend, putting on a summer-weight suit that was really meant for fall; something she could get into and out of easily. But even as she dressed, her day settled, planned, she had that persistent feeling of unrest. Damn Joan anyway! And damn Ernie, too. Well, she would simply call him until she reached him, or was told he had left town.

On several occasions he had declared that he had never had a relationship like this one, not with anybody; and in his juvenile wistfulness had said, "No matter what happens, we'll always be friends, won't we?" and Peggy had assured him that they would. Even at the time she had made a mental reservation, however, and, as if she were a child, too, wishing on a star, hoped to herself that it would come true. But it wouldn't come true if the raw material of the dreamlife they shared was made out of the tissue substance of lies. Well, she would see.

Checking the time as she went out the door, she called to Mamie that she didn't know when she'd be back exactly, but would call in.

"How about dinner?" Mamie wanted to know.

Peggy hesitated. "I'll be here, and maybe Mr. Marvin, too," she said.

Mamie's disapproval was almost audible as Peggy left.

Downstairs, the doorman, as usual, was unsuccessful in getting her a cab, so she walked to the corner and got one for herself. She gave the driver the address of the restaurant uptown where she was meeting Ab, then leaned her head back against the hot, imitation leather and thought: At seven-thirty this morning I was in another world; in a world of four air-tight walls as impervious to the currents of the rest of civilization as a desert island. And now, here I am, off that island, running my fool head off, and paying dearly for my escape. Full of dreads and doubts, lies and evasions purling off my tongue as if they were all my brain could feed it. She sighed, and thought of her long untouched literary project, and, once again envied her so productive brother on the West Coast who was adding to his wealth by his wits, while she…. She shook her head. I must not be depressed, she thought. If I see Ernie tonight—if he *is* in town—I must be light and gay, full of amusing anecdotes of the day. Where the hell, she thought glumly, shall I find amusing anecdotes for this day?

As it turned out, this was a very good question. Nothing she tried on fit. She remembered, while struggling out of a little number as airless as it was sleeveless, that she had switched her hairdresser's appointment until this afternoon, and had to rush to make it. While there, above the hum of the dryers, sounding more like machines in a sugar mill than a beauty factory, she called Ernie once more. It was long after two; he had left for the day. "Will he be in tomorrow?" she asked anxiously, and was told yes, as far as they knew, he would.

"That swine," she said aloud into the safe roar of the hair machines, then afforded herself the undetected luxury of bowing her head and trying to cry. But the keening attempt hit dry rock, and, recovering, she inserted another dime in the pay phone, even while her name was being called to come back, they were ready for her shampoo. All the same, she let the phone at his apartment ring nine times, two over her customary seven, dictated by polite custom and the phone company, before she returned to the booth to get her hair washed.

While she was mechanically passing Mr. Leon the big plastic rollers with which he was setting her hair, she remembered, with some glad anticipation, that she had completely forgotten until now to check with Mamie and the answering service. Of course! Ernie would have called there. Where else?

As soon as her hair was up, netted, and Mr. Leon was trying to stick her under a dryer, she made for the telephone once more. Mamie was out marketing, so it was Louise who answered.

"No'm I'm sure you didn't get no call from Mr. Marvin," Louise insisted. "I knows his voice. But you did get a telegraph."

"Oh?" said Peggy. "Read it to me, will you?"

Louise excused herself to go get her glasses. When she came back, there was much ripping open of the envelope and rattling of paper as she got it rightside up. "ARRIVING IDLEWILD. BOAC FLIGHT 707. FIVE P.M. E.D.T."

"Oh, my God!" Peggy breathed. "Anything else?"

"No'm, just a 'T.' Reckon that stands for Mr. Tom?"

"Yeah, I reckon, Louise," said Peggy as she hurriedly consulted her watch. It was four-ten. With luck she would barely make it.

CHAPTER TWENTY-NINE

E HAD just hung up the phone after talking with Al Gehmann and was on his way in to see Claude about the new report, when his secretary caught him. "Another call, Ern. On four."

As he went towards the instrument he raised his eyebrows significantly in unspoken question as to the sex of the caller; the girl nodded, indicating female. "Tell her I'm out," Ernie said silent-movie style, but the woman had turned her head and was answering a question put to her by the bookkeeper.

Oh, what the hell, thought Ernie as he picked up the phone, I can always tell her the trip's been postponed until after lunch; or make her think I said after lunch in the first place. "Hello," he said in his usual short-cut slightly aggressive manner.

"Hello to you," a woman's lilting voice came back, one that for the moment he couldn't place.

"Yep. Hello," he said succinctly, still not recognizing his caller. If there was anything he disliked it was telephonic guessing games during office hours.

"Has it been that long, Ernie?" the woman's voice said, half teasing, half yearning.

"Hi, ducks," he said, knowing now who it was. "It has indeed. When are you free for lunch?"

"In about fifteen minutes."

"Umm hmm," Ernie said, looking at his wristwatch. "Fine. Where?"

"How about Michael's Pub?" said she.

Ernie frowned. It was expensive and the phoney English tavern atmosphere got on his nerves. "You need reservations."

"I don't," Joan laughed. "Remember? That's one of my favorite lunching places."

"Oh, yes," said Ernie quietly; he had known there was some reason he didn't like it.

"Then around twelve-fifteen, twelve-thirty?"

"Make it teen," he said. "I have to be back in the office early and get out this report—even if it takes all night."

"What a thought!" Joan cried gaily.

As he hung up he wondered what she was sounding so cheerful about. Betsy reported she had seemed quite quiet these days, which, for usually easygoing, often exuberant Joan, was equivalent to being morose. But maybe she was just excited at the prospect of seeing him. It was possible. His babes, he had found, didn't recover from him so easily. He had known them to trail him for years, dragging the torch behind them. Just this morning, for instance, he had had still another letter from Angeline, begging him to come rescue her from West Virginia. And Gloria, his old girl from three summers ago, had certainly sounded all worked up when he had called her to set up a dinner date for tonight. But tomorrow night, for sure, he would go home, have an early quiet dinner of pork and beans, or something easy out of a can, and at last start this report. And on Wednesday or Thursday he planned to spend the evening with Charlotte and Hank—during the course of which Hank could be counted upon to discreetly absent himself, of course. Better make it Wednesday if possible, he decided, for on Friday he would be saddled with *her* again.

Why, he asked himself, did he think that way about Peggy when he was away from her? He didn't know. With her, he was contented, if not perfectly happy, boiling over with bliss; she suited him somehow, with her quiet manner, her thoughtful ways, her ebullient small wit and easygoing, but sharp sense about everything. So why did she bore and oppress him in retrospect? It was very strange. Maybe because she *was* too good to him and for him. He had tried many times to start an impassioned argument with her: usually it ended in a formal, reasoning argument, as stiff with logic as a classroom philosopher's, or else it took a legal bent. Only twice had they ended up in a tussle— biting and scratching and kicking, chasing each other all over the small apartment. That had been rather nice. But that wasn't it either. What he wanted, he supposed, was someone built along the lines of Joan, who did her screaming and biting and moaning in bed, and who was as socially decorative and bright as Peggy in the drawing room. And, preferably, a woman who did NOT drink! Peggy had been absolutely potted three nights last week. He had even been ashamed to be seen with her in Fanny's, and, God knows, that was going pretty far. She told him that she had been drinking like this ever since her first marriage broke up.

Well, all he could say was that it could happen again—and again, and again. On top of which, the woman was simply too cloying. She knew thousands of people, why did she have to wait around for him? And he knew she did wait. He wondered what had been on her mind when she called him this morning? Wanted to know, Elizabeth had said, if he had left town yet. Yes, wouldn't she like to know. But he rather thought she had called for some purpose or other; he had more or less broken her of the habit of calling to make idle chitchat—and even if she had had no purpose motivating her she was clever enough to have invented one. Oh, she knew him pretty well in some areas. If his schedule had not been so full for the next few days, he would have called her to find out what had been on her mind. But he couldn't. He couldn't say to her: Look here, darling, I've got some other dates this week. You run along and play with your little friends and I'll play with mine.

Why he couldn't say this, he didn't exactly know; he certainly had in the beginning and she had taken it equitably enough. But, somehow, fibbing had come to seem easier, better, even though the one or two times she had caught him out she had made him see that her anger (quite justifiable, he had to admit) was not at all jealousy inspired, but was the disrespect and discourtesy of being lied to. He had apologized, promised not to do it again, but was secretly peeved at her in turn for having made him feel thoroughly meek. These sweet-looking, small women could be as domineering as the big ones, such as his mother had been.

In any event, he thought as he walked smartly down Madison, dodging some giggling office girls bobbing their beehive hairdos in mirth, in order to make the light without jaywalking, in any event, he wished Tom would come back and drain off some of her excess time, or that she would reattach herself to that arty yet snobby crowd of rich people she had tried to interest him in in the beginning. He had, he knew, been quite impressed—by a few of them he'd been overwhelmed; Western money wasn't like New York or Eastern money. These people were far better dressed than Betsy's Denver crowd, even if they didn't show their money off with airplanes and horses and sprawling paneled ranchhouses. No, Peggy's pals were all good-looking, complicated, worldly, knowing, brittle—there was nothing sweet and simple about them, with the possible exception of a few of their minds. But they weren't clannish either—which was Betsy's substitute out West for snobbish—though they did seem to think it was pretty depressing if you didn't have much money. They had it and just forgot about it, that's all.

How I'd like to go back to Europe again, he was thinking as he entered the restaurant, winding up his thoughts. Maybe, if I play it right with dear Peggy....

Then he caught sight of Joan.

CHAPTER THIRTY

J OAN, IN a black raw silk sheath (which was probably the one Betsy had mentioned having cost $200), and wearing a very becoming hat with a floppy brim, took off her sunglasses when she saw him, gave him her white-gloved hand and a most becoming smile.

"You look lovely, darling," he said appreciatively, taking her in. "Been waiting long?"

"No," she said, "just seconds," though he noticed that her whiskey sour glass was drained quite dry, and that the fruit had been nibbled down to the rind and stem respectively.

She had been sitting at one of the little tables opposite the bar, and now she stood up, replaced her dark glasses and said, "I think we can go in any time. He has a table for us and I assured him you would be absolutely on time—and you were, just like my old lover-boy that I remembered."

This sounded a trifle sarcastic to Ernie, but he supposed he was in for some needling anyway; it was one of the prices you had to pay for field-playing independence.

He followed along behind Joan, who, in her high-heeled black patent leather shoes, seemed as tall as Betsy—i.e., rather towering, rather overpowering. That was one thing about Angeline, and Peggy, too, for that matter....

"... Is this all right, sir?" he realized the waiter was saying, already half pulling the table away from the booth so that they could get in.

"Will this do us, darling?" Joan echoed.

"Splendid," Ernie told the man with his usual crisp dignity, reserved for such people.

Joan looked over the menu as she absently drew off her gloves. "Oh, God," she said to herself, remembering to take off her dark glasses. She could feel her shoulders begin to wilt—she had been up forever, it seemed—and consciously sat up straight. "Well, darling," she said brightly, her smile as unforced and genuinely alert as she could make it. "What will you have?"

For a moment, it seemed that Joan was determined to order for them, but then she recalled herself and Ernie took over. He took pride in the clarity and precision with which he ordered food, or gave instructions in general to underlings. And he did not like being deprived of the privilege; he didn't even like this prerogative threatened, so he felt slightly out of sorts with Joan.

She continued to look at him brightly, but there was a cryptic expression lurking around her eyes, of mischief, perhaps, fun-poking, if not something worse. In turn, as if challenging, he smirked at her, so that in the end they were each staring at the other, not absorbed in study, but like two children who have a dare to see which one will blink first.

Joan decided it was politic to blink first. After all, she *really* had something on her mind, and could well afford to be womanly demure with him. She idly began to flop her gloves up and down on the table, a little gesture that evoked Ernie's intense displeasure. Besides, the gloves were simply filthy.

But Joan wasn't thinking; or, rather, she was thinking thoughts far elsewhere, for before she had finally got Ernie on the phone a plan had come into her head—a heavenly, probably foolproof plan for getting him back; and for always. So sure of it she had been, that she had lost no time in dressing and had taken a taxi directly to the building on Madison and 50th where he worked and had called him from the lobby; that's why she was early at Michael's Pub. While waiting, sipping her whiskey sour, she had perfected this plan. All that remained now was its delivery, and this, she had decided, was going to be slow, artless, at first, then flowering into a masterpiece of gradually applied pressure, until the pain would be excruciating: then let him writhe and squirm. "You're looking well after all your travels," she said. "I see you still haven't lost your summer tan."

"Tennis," he gestured and smiled at her genially.

"Oh? With Hank still?"

"Occasionally. He belongs to a tennis club."

"Tennis and Racquet?" Joan asked bitchily.

"Who do you think you're lunching with?" he decided to squelch her at once. "A Persian cat?"

She laughed her head off. "No. Alley, darling. You left yourself wide-open for that one. Anyway, why shouldn't Hank Adams belong to the Tennis and Racquet Club? After all, isn't he Henry Adams the umpteenth or something?"

"No reason," he said levelly, "except your implication seemed to be you might know one."

She shrugged elaborately.

He gave her a look of contempt, open enough to be ten miles out to sea. "Look here, Joan. What's all this act? Just because you've got yourself out of those summer dungarees and into VOGUE's idea of autumn vogue, you don't have to smarten up the inside of your head, too. It doesn't go with you, sweetie. On you it hangs like a sack."

"You mean to tell me I'm dumb?" she demanded in surprise and anger. It was beyond her to interpret this as a physical criticism.

"Not dumb, sweetie. But that artificial, affected smartness is just—well, it's artificial. You sound like you're trying to ape your friend Peggy, or somebody."

"Or Betsy, perhaps?" she said with a slight frostiness, and her attempt at a snarl Ernie found downright pathetic. She'd better do some more practising in the mirror before she tried that on the *haute monde* again.

"Okay, so you think I'm a swine."

"One of Peggy's words, I see," she said narrowly.

"Oh, is it?"

She smiled at this as if she couldn't help herself, and didn't mind in any case. Now, he thought, maybe she's ready to let me out of the pillory.

"Well, let's begin over then, Ernie. I really have missed you, you know."

Yes, he knew; and he let her take one of his hands in hers, making her think, in his adroit way, that the impulse to do so had been his. "I've missed you, too, sweetie," he murmured, turning all the soulful searchlight power of his one eye upon her.

She closed her eyes expressively, and, to be sure, two small trickles started from them. "We mustn't, Ernie, we must *not* just drift away from each other," she said, biting her lip, then opened her eyes again. But she kept her face half averted.

"No use to cry, ducks," he said. "We're here now, aren't we?"

"How's Betsy these days, Ernie—*really?*" she said with a change of subject, as smart as a military about-face.

"You see her fairly often," he said neutrally. "You tell me.

Joan shook her head and looked troubled. "Sometimes, Ernie, I think you two should get a divorce."

"Oh, we make out all right," he said leisurely.

"I just hope Betsy agrees with you."

"Betsy hasn't complained to me—not lately," he said, purposely making the statement sound as if something significant were implied.

BONNIE GOLIGHTLY

Their round of drinks at last came, and momentarily, this shifted the nature of the conversation. Primarily because Joan wanted fruit in her whiskey sour, and it had been left out; she having been mistaken for a lady of fashion.

When the fruit was duly inserted and they were drinking away again (seconds ordered), Joan resumed her campaign. "By the way, Ernie, I said something to Peggy about coming to dinner on Friday and she said she had a date with you—so is it all right if you two dine with us? You can go on later if you have something else on for that evening."

"Delighted," Ernie assured her instantly—so quickly that had she known him as closely and well as she had had vast opportunity for doing, she would have been on guard. But as Ernie had no rattlers, she wasn't aware that he was about to strike.

"I do hope," she said with a charming, only slightly misfitting smile of coquetry for her large mouth, "that you and Peggy aren't—shall we say, involved with each other?"

"Do you mean, do we have sexual intercourse? Certainly. Don't you and Bill? Shall I go on and include every adult of our mutual acquaintance—yes, including myself and Betsy?"

"I don't believe it," she murmured stunned into despair.

He gave her a short harsh laugh. "About me and Betsy, or about Peggy?"

She wanted to say, I don't believe either, but she stayed mum and rather frightened.

"However, as for being 'involved' with Peggy, to quote you, I'd like you to be explicit—providing you *had* anything more explicit in mind than our sexual habits."

"I think those are pretty general enough," Joan said lifelessly, still terribly downcast.

"Oh, come off it, darling," he suddenly put his hand over hers and tried to look into her eyes. "All right. So Peggy and I

140

tried it once. It didn't work. And now we are occasional dinner companions—when I'm in town," he added, firmly believing that an afterthought, no matter how tardily delivered, is better than none, and will serve as a sop to those who want it.

But with Joan it had just the opposite effect: it simply gave her another bullet for her bombardment of questions, delivered in a volley so quick that he laughed in spite of himself and asked her to slow down. And, too, this had the advantage of letting him stall for time.

"But you *do* have an apartment in town," she said sorrowfully. "You could have asked me up, now and again." The tears, he noticed, were coming out once more.

"You, darling? Do you consider yourself the sort of woman a man wants to make matinee love to, or an occasional stolen night?" Even as he delivered this gallant, manly speech, he was aware that he was making an awful gaff—after all, what had he and Joan had, but just such brief encounters? He hoped she wouldn't notice.

Either she didn't, or was so carried away on wings of love that she merely sighed deeply, and, pledging with her eyes, said, "Ernie, I am so insane about you—yes, still—that—that I have no pride. I'd take you any way I could, since our plan to be together wasn't to be."

Ernie gave her a sunless smile and patted her hand. "It will all work out, ducks. See if it doesn't."

"I hope so, Ernie. Oh, how I hope so. I have no course but to trust you—"

"Oh?" he said. "That's a new wrinkle," and laughed at his own doomed attempt at a feeble joke.

"I know you can't keep away from women—you never could—and they can't keep away from you, but I just hope the girl you have living there—"

"I have no one living there," he interrupted brusquely.

"Well, if you're playing around, then, I just hope those girls won't mind your spending a little more time with me. Because you see, Ernie," she heaved a sigh, "I'm going to need you. Very much."

"You got cancer or something?" he asked in light scorn. He was finding her PTA histrionics, as brought to bear on the romantic-love in-heat syndrome, itchy-crawly and wearing.

She shook her head, and now the tear faucets were on full blast. Thank God, however, the woman had taught herself how to cry without making any noise—the least, of course, she could do with such a doubtful talent. "No, sweetie, something worse and something beautifully better, at the same time," she said at last, the plumbing cut off, though there were a few sniffs left.

"You mean you're pregnant," he said, as if it were a stock line from a tenth-rate play.

"That's right," she said, clearing her nasal passage in a piece of disintegrating Kleenex. "In a way I couldn't be more pleased. Bill, of course, thinks it's his—and it's so lovely that it's not. You know, Ernie, I think even before I—I *knew* you—you know what I mean—back even then, I think I used to wish to myself I could have such a father for a child of mine. He'll be so beautiful—"

"And so dumb," Ernie added with a smile, but it was all a smile of pleasure. His pride was as tall as a mountain.

CHAPTER THIRTY-ONE

S O PLEASED was Ernie, in fact, that he himself suggested taking the rest of the afternoon off—a thing he never did, being a conscientious compulsive, and liking his job—in order to "show her the apartment." They both understood this euphemism so well that she was already undressed and in one of the twin beds—the one he had indicated—when he came into the bedroom bearing gins and tonics on a tray. Seeing her lying there like that, the sheets thrown back, he knew there was no time for gin and tonic; in fact, there was just barely time for him to take his clothes off.

He made rapturous love to her, steady, inflamed, almost too quick, but of course not quite, or he would have been unable to quip, when it was over, "Hmmm. Instant love."

She laughed at him happily, and pushed him away. "All sticky," was her comment as she rose on her elbow.

"It'll be better next time," he promised, his smile at her all for her, in a way it had never been before. "You know," he announced, leaning back and taking a critical look at her, "I now understand why Bill is so hung up on those Modigliani nudes."

"You mean you never noticed before, you swine?"

"Watch out," he teased, "that's Peggy's word, remember?" and dodged as she made a playful swipe at him.

They were both having a very good time.

He got out of bed and handed her a gin and tonic. "Here's to Ernest Roche," he said, and took a swallow, then commented, "Gosh, it seems a shame to have a child of mine named Roche."

"Well, it's too late now," Joan returned lightly. She knew better than to think Ernie was working up to a proposal of mutual divorce to culminate in their marriage.

"How late is it?" he asked.

"It happened the last time, apparently," she said, smiling up at him in a relaxed fond way. "I'll bet lots of babies are conceived at Montauk."

"Why? Because of all the phallic symbols out there?"

"Well, I could name a few," she said a little wickedly.

"Joan," he said, putting an emphatic hand on her thigh, "you're a good old girl."

"Yes, so they say," she sighed.

"You know," he said on impulse, "Peggy likes you a lot."

"Oh?" she said eyeing him, cooler now.

"Don't you like Peggy anymore?"

"I don't know as I really do, come to think of it. I'm prejudiced, of course, where you're concerned. But then the gnat-brained way she has acted about keeping Tom—"

"Maybe Tom's had it."

"And who could blame him?" Joan asked archly.

"I don't mean that. I mean 'had it,' as in had his day."

"You think so?" she asked casually, but he could feel her interest, jealousy—or womanly intuition, as she would have called it—stirring faintly.

"I don't know," he backed away from the subject. "You know her, I don't. And I've never even met him."

Inadvertently, as he reached over to take her empty glass from her hand, his arm brushed across her breast. She shivered in ecstasy and held out her arms.

He didn't much want to, so soon, and it was awkward disposing of her glass before he joined her, but he did. And while the fire of desire was no longer the frenzied thing, heightened like a blaze with kerosene poured on it, it was a fire, nonetheless, and a quite satisfactory one, duly quenched in good order and in good time.

As he released himself from her, lay there panting—it really was still too hot for this sort of thing without air conditioning or an electric fan—the phone rang.

Joan made a move toward it; she always answered phones, no matter where they rang.

"No, no!" he said sternly and pushed her back.

She stared at him in amazement, then, "But aren't you going to answer it?"

"No," he said tight-jawed.

"But what's the point in having a phone if you don't answer it?"

"It came with the apartment and it's good for outgoing calls."

She was silent a second, then ventured, "Not for me, it wasn't."

"Give me a chance," he said harshly. "Besides, things are rather different now."

They listened together, their shoulders drooping, their faces sagging with fatigue and emptiness, as the phone went on until it had rung itself out.

"Persistent lady," Joan commented, looking at the wall and tracing a finger along it.

"Obviously," he said, clipping the word.

"Anybody I should know?" she asked, casting a look at him.

"I don't see any reason why you should know Gloria," he told her, still not quite recovered from the strident clarion of the telephone bell: it had almost had the effect of an air-raid signal on their merriment. Then his ease returned. "Gloria is a babe I used to make it with a long time ago—really a stupid girl, but not bad to look at and quite superb in bed—no, duckie," he cast a fond look at Joan, "nowhere near your match—but after the music died, so to speak, she liked to use me as *mentor inamorata*—" he smiled at her, and she gave him a warm one back, despite his bold and inadmissible Latin. "So," he continued, "every time this babe gets a new boyfriend, she comes to me for advice."

"Tell me, Ernie. Do you call all your women babes?"

"No," he said beginning to break into mirth in that familiar way that told he was about to say something funny, "but I call all my babes women!"

"Watch out, there!" she warned playfully. "I know of a little fellow who'll be coming along pretty soon who won't like that."

"Suppose he's a girl?"

"Then we'll call her Babe, in your honor."

"Helluva name for a girl," he murmured, squeezing her hand.

"But heavenly for a woman, huh?" she asked, looking into his profile, and squeezing his hand back.

They were still lying down, arms entwined, much as he and Peggy had lain that morning, only in the other bed, across the room. From the way the sun slanted across the blinds and struck the counterpane of the bed beneath it, Joan knew it was awfully late. But just then the phone began its ringing again, only this time it was not so alarming, so soul-chilling. Again, Ernie let it ring itself out.

"Do you have a date with this Gloria girl tonight?" Joan inquired. "If that's who it is, I don't see why you don't answer."

"Maybe she'll think I'm out of town," he turned to her with a conspiratorial smile. "I had thought I might be all last week."

"Oh, you swine!" she cried back at him for the twinkle of mischief in his eye. Then her grin subsided to a smile. "That 'swine' thing is handy, isn't it?" she asked. "Peggy or no Peggy."

"No Peggy. And anyway, I tell you she has graduated to scoundrel."

"You must be awful with her, in that case."

"A foul fiend," he assured her.

This rather Biblical-sounding wrath-of-God cliche seemed to have an effect on her. "You know, Ernie," she said after a time, "much as I want this baby, I can't help but think it's a terrible thing to do to poor Bill."

"Why?" Ernie immediately contended. "The child, as you say, will undoubtedly be handsome and well-formed, if not necessarily downright beautiful—but that's a strong possibility, too. And intelligent, and besides, Bill is rich. He's also a nice guy and deserves to have one exemplary child grace his home."

"You conceited, insulting—" she spluttered.

"Isn't it true that my children are better looking and smarter than your present ones?"

"Oh, Ernie, how can you say such a thing to me? And even if I weren't their mother, even if I didn't love them for that reason, I'm not so sure that I could go any further than to say that all those kids are so different! How can you possibly compare?"

"I can," he said stonily. "I *know* my kids are exceedingly different. Outstandingly so. Paul is a genius, and Diedre is nearly so."

"Oh, darling, do be sensible! I'm a parent too. Who told you this, for instance? Of course, they're unusually bright children—"

"Unusually bright?" he whipped on her furiously. "The testing centers in East Hampton *and* Montclair declared them geniuses."

Joan looked at him sadly, "Sweetie, I won't run those places down, but I will say that even if the NYU Testing Clinic, Ethical Culture, the Mayo Clinic and Freud all declared them geniuses, it would still only mean genius potential—"

"I hope your child is subnormal," he said in shaking fury. "It would serve you right, and it would especially serve Bill right!"

CHAPTER THIRTY-TWO

I T TOOK Ernie longer than usual to come out of the heat and ague of his anger, and the whiteness of it lingered in his face. Joan felt touched and concerned; she had not known he was so violent and illogical on the subject of his fatherhood, but, in a way, she could understand. Finally, she left, though Ernie begged her to stay, saying that he was going to stand up his date anyway, being in no mood to see anyone but her, but Joan said, "Sweet, dear, one of us must be sensible," and after looking into his eye with a warm, reassuring smile, and clasping his hand, she left him, even without a kiss.

Even as he was seeing her out the door, she heard the telephone ringing again. My, that girl was persistent. But by the time Joan was outside in the street, it had stopped—or he had answered it. Poor Ernie. Poor, dear trusting Ernie. And now, she could acknowledge it: she felt a little ashamed of herself. Only it had seemed such a good idea at the time, schoolgirl trick or not, and besides, it wasn't as simple as that. Joan had had so much trouble with her menstrual periods—all of her life, really, and after the babies they had seemed to get even more irregular, if possible—that she had thought nothing of it when she skipped all of August, September, and now. So she *could* be pregnant—that's the way the other two had happened—a two months' skip, a rabbit test in the third month, and then the word—neither good nor bad, but of mixed blessings. For, she felt convinced, neither she nor Bill had been psychologically ready.

But this time she was ready, curiously enough, and she didn't have the faintest idea, at this moment, whose child, if any, it might be. Oh, she supposed she could work it out, thanks to that engagement calendar Bill kept on his desk, in which he noted down all their "social events" (and what better gauge for remembering sexual couplings were there than social events? You either violently did or you violently didn't). So Joan was pretty sure she could tell. In any event, she would hie herself off to her doctor tomorrow, get rabbit tests, "soundings,"—as a friend of hers called them, in a rather quaint humorous way—and then she would know.

But she had not liked that closing remark he had made about Bill; about a subnormal child serving Bill right. Not that she had liked the other remarks either, but, thanks to Bill who knew so much about these things, she, too, could calmly sympathize with Ernie's small, but pervasive neurosis—so long as she stayed with Bill, as she fully intended to do. Safe and sound and sane, his hand holding hers, guiding her. How awful it must be, she thought, to actually be married to Ernie! It had been Joan's own husband who had made that famous remark when someone was suggesting analysis might help Ernie. "What?" Bill had said in mock gravity and concern. "Ernie go into *analysis!* Does Lawrence of Arabia consult Freud?"

It had been too screamingly funny, for all of them there at the time had been only too familiar with Ernie's own contradictory bragging accounts of his exploits in field and stream, bed and board, in war and in peace. The original little tin soldier. Yes, alas, one had to laugh at Ernie a little.

Then Joan began to worry. Suppose she were pregnant and the child was his, would it inherit Ernie's instability? My God, what a thought!

Finally she spied a taxi with a light on top, and it stopped for her. She practically shivered, warm as it was, all the way home, wishing she could remember more about the laws of heredity from her college psychology course. Of course she could ask Bill—he would know, as he knew practically everything—but she had no ready excuse—not tonight anyway—for wanting to know, and, in the circumstances, she hated to invent one. If she did find out in a few days, after the A-Z test, that she was pregnant, she could ask then. Or she could even go to the public library, though she was not sure she would still know how to look things up, it had been so long since she had availed herself of such informational facilities. Let's face it, she thought, I'm soft and even a little stupid. And I'm certainly wantonly irresponsible ... at my time of life, a wife with a good husband, a mother of three lovely kids ... how dare I present all of them with an unknown quantity to cope with and adjust to? It was bad enough to have lost her head and fallen for the biggest little prick in and *out* of Greater New York.

Tears of contrition bathed her face, but it was too late, too late.... Bill would never hear to her having an abortion; as a matter of fact, he rather wanted a fourth child. And of course she could never admit to him that she had been unfaithful, that the child might not be his. She couldn't even bear to think of such a thing, much less plot out the consequences. No, if she was pregnant, she was stuck with it. And what about Ernie? Oh, her trick had worked, all right! Only too well. From now on, if she liked, she could be court favorite, Number One Wife away from Wife. But who needed it? And that stuffy little apartment, sneaking up there two or three times a week to make love.... She had to remind herself that just that morning this act had seemed to her the most deliciously desirable thing she could ever attain. Well ... he was attractive, and when the cold weather came, the apartment wouldn't really be so bad. Then, too, Ernie took such obvious pleasure in her—he always had in her body—and now this precious gift of life which she would bear, making up, she could see and understand now, for all the bitter frustration he had had when Betsy's organs were removed. Yes, in having this baby she would be executing the Golden Rule to the letter, for all hands concerned.

She smiled to herself, feeling happy and hopeful again; her old self. There was great satisfaction to be derived in giving pleasure to others.

CHAPTER THIRTY-THREE

P EGGY'S HAIR was not quite dry, but this concerned Mr. Leon far more than it did her as she kept urging him to comb it out faster, saying that it didn't matter how it looked.

"But you're meeting your *husband!*" he protested mournfully. "For the husband every woman must look even *better* than she really is!"

"I must remember that," Peggy commented dryly, quite fed up with Gallic sagacity for the moment, but Mr. Leon gave her a little understanding nod, indicating his gratitude at finding that she was wise enough to appreciate what he told her, even if she were an impetuous American female, incapable of following her wits.

She sped out of the shop at exactly four-thirty, and somehow arrived at Idlewild at five (her watch had been fast). Now she slowed down; if the plane was already in, Tom would still be a few minutes in customs. She strolled to the BOAC desk and was told the plane was thirty minutes late.

This news Peggy received with many glad tidings; for thirty minutes, if necessary, she could devote herself to the telephone with Ernie. Promptly she found a phone booth and called the number. Again, no answer. Exasperating. She bought a magazine, tried to read that for ten minutes, called again. The line was busy. This smote her a cruel blow, then after the blinding hurt of it passed (how *could* he sit there and let her ring and ring without answering, then turn around and answer someone else's call, or place one himself?), she got an inspiration, quick and brilliant as lightning. She'd have the operator check the line to see if it really was busy (talking), out of order (impossible), or engaged because someone else was dialing the number, too (which she hoped was the case). But, of course, by the time the operator did as she was bidden the line was as free as a bird, and the piercing little intermittent rings performed upon it went on and on and would have done so forever had Peggy not received the message that the phone was in order, but did not answer.

Peggy was truly downcast after this, and thoroughly confused. Where could he be? she asked herself disconsolately. First, he had told her he was going out of town; but then he *hadn't* gone out of town. Or had he? No. He had said the trip was business, so of course his office would know. Then why had he lied to her? Or had he lied to her? Hadn't his trips sometimes been canceled before? But if this was the case, why hadn't he phoned her? And he hadn't, no, he hadn't, she bitterly told herself. She must keep at least that fact in mind. He had not called her. For whatever reason, he had not called her. Maybe, she thought, discovering a new straw she hadn't tried as yet to have and hold, maybe he had to go to Montclair suddenly; something wrong with one of the children. Yes, that was likely. Probably exactly what had happened. All the same, she decided, I'll try phoning him at the apartment just once more, then it will be time for Tom's plane.

She returned to the booth, her feet under her like dead weights to be dragged along. This was her last chance. Last chance for gas before the desert. The unknown. She put the dime in the slot, wondering exactly what she would do—or say—if miraculously she got him this time. One couldn't very well say, "Save me!" The dial went round and round, spinning toward its destination. She held her breath as it whirled, watching as if it were a roulette wheel upon which her fortune, her very life were staked. The digits delivered, the mechanism clicked and prepared itself for ringing. One short experimental ring, then the quick, even staccato of the busy signal. The line was busy! Impossible! Quickly she dialed again. Busy. Then again. Still busy. Then, to give him a chance to finish talking and—hope against hope— to find out if he had phoned her, she called her own apartment. Mamie this time. Was Mr. Tom in yet? Not yet. They'd be home directly afterwards. Yes, just the two of them for dinner, but— had Mr. Marvin called? Indeed he had not. Mamie's much too bossy, Peggy thought to herself as she quickly put a new dime in the slot and dialed Ernie's number. When it still flashed that ugly, rude, unceasing little noise in her ear which told her it was busy, she could have cried. Just once more, she thought, glancing at her watch. Just once more, for she was sure by this time Tom's plane was certainly on the ground, and if he wasn't already through customs and looking for her, she would be lucky. Well, let him wait, she thought angrily, *I've* waited long enough for him, or let him take a cab into town. She dialed the phone in an emphatic fury, as if this would make it mind her, make it work. Still busy.

She rose from the booth, quietly gathered her pocketbook and magazine and strolled toward the area where one could see the passengers, wave to them as they went through customs, before the joyful reunion took place. Anyone seeing her graceful carriage, the poised way she held her head, the slight smile on her lips would have thought her a contented, well-adjusted pretty young woman, out here, perhaps, for the purpose of welcoming a cousin, someone else's brother, or a delegate to a convention, for her eyes were far too cool and grave for excitement or happiness.

She caught sight of Tom about the same time as he saw her, and they exchanged cheerful, friendly waves. She watched him as he progressed along the line. He had his trenchcoat—his war-correspondent's badge—still slung over his arm, just as he had

had it when he left; maybe he had been out here all this time, had never gone to England or anywhere at all. Staring down at him, it didn't even occur to her to wonder, or feel hurt, that after their casual greeting he had not looked once in her direction. He was going about his business with his usual dispatch, exactly as if he were entering a city where he had no friends, knew no one. Well, she thought to herself, curiously enough, coincidentally enough, he is in a strange, friendless city. He certainly can't count on me for any warmth. He might as well be a stone, as might I. But he looked pleasant enough. He had grown another mustache, she noticed; seemed quite becoming this time, now that she was more objective, she supposed. And his hair was as bright and well groomed as ever. What woman wouldn't be delighted to be married to this very tall, good-looking blond man? So sure of himself; so right; and such a fool—

It was then that she simply turned on her heel, walked down the flight of stairs, outside the building, and, without a backward glance, got into a waiting cab and gave him Ernie's address.

CHAPTER THIRTY-FOUR

ERNIE SUPPOSED that in retrospect this day would be extremely titillating—sexually exciting, too; useful for onanism as well as poker evenings and stag parties, but right now he was just plain tired, and he wished Gloria would leave him alone. He had been out of his mind to suggest that she come here first, instead of his picking her up, but anything to get her off the phone. And even then, after that interminable conversation—all useless if he was to see her anyway—he had been still half convinced that what he had told Joan was the truth: that he didn't want to see Gloria or anybody, and that he would stand her up. It would have been perfectly simple to turn off all the lights, and not answer the door. But then he hadn't, had he? And the inevitable had happened: as soon as she hit the door she wanted to hit the sack. And here she was. And ready for seconds, yet.

"Not now, sweetie," he murmured and lay on his back, a thin line of space separating her big not very appetizing body from him; a line he had created with great surreptitious care. He didn't exactly want to hurt the creature's feelings, but this was absolutely the last time. Final. And as soon as he got her persuaded back into her clothes, taken out somewhere and fed, installed in a taxi, and the taxi door slammed, that would be it for her; her little slice of foreverness.

All right, call it spoiled, if you like, but everybody has a right to upgrade the line. And, discounting money, brains, social position, accomplishment, style—almost anything in the realm of acquisitions—both Joan and Peggy, not to mention Charlotte and a few others, had it all over this babe. Beside her they were simply luscious. All poor Gloria really had to recommend her were a pair of hot pants. And they might as well have been of cast iron, too, for all the sexiness she generated. She was one of those girls who never got enough and never gave anything. Making love to her—how could he so denigrate the expression?—was like that old saw about the potato sack. The moral to this conquest, he supposed, was that every nympho is not a nymph. And sorry that she was there beside him in this bed where he had lain with Joan was no word for it.

"You ready again, dearie?" she laid one rather rough-skinned large hand boldly upon him.

"No," he said irritably, instantly changing his position to his side to avoid being further used or contacted by her hand. "I'm asleep."

"Well, pardon me for living," she said airily, affecting annoyance. But none she could affect, none she could actually feel, could match his; moreover, nothing she could do could move him from his present dispassion. And, if she continued, he knew he would get downright rude, in spite of himself.

How he wished that little fabrication he had given Joan about Gloria had been the truth! How he wished indeed that this ungainly slob had boyfriend problems—other than her own with him—which he could neatly, expeditiously solve!

But here, too, as everywhere, it seemed, he was "the man in her life." And he had asked her, as he had asked all of them, great and small, beautiful and ugly, sexy and frigid, smart and dumb: "What do you see in me?" And not one of them had ever been able to tell him. He knew well enough what he saw in them, could tell them in a trice—

He suddenly froze. The outside bell, it was ringing ... persistently. He put a silent restraining hand on Gloria's rough hide, and listened as the bell rang on and on. It was nobody ringing every bell in the house, trying to get in because of lost or forgotten keys, or even to housebreak—that was certain. Whoever was ringing was ringing *here,* for *him,* and they weren't going to like no for an answer. But no was what they were going to get, nonetheless. He wouldn't have answered that bell, pressed that buzzer, for a million dollars.

"Won't it never stop?" his companion whispered at his side.

"Shhh!" he said harshly, not at all aware that the grasp he had on her thigh was brutally hard.

Then, at last, the ringing stopped. He moaned slightly, unaware of this too, and ran his hand down his side; it was slithery, encased in sweat.

"Me too," she said, observing his discovery of his condition. "Why don't we jump in a shower?"

"Shhh!" he commanded in furious stage whisper. "Don't you know she may still be out there?"

"Who?" asked Gloria, using for the sake of injury and defiance a voice register just slightly under her normal one.

"My wife!" he retorted.

"Well, you don't hardly have no call to take it out on me," she remarked in her still offended tone.

"You don't realize how serious this is," he said, climbing over her to get out of bed. He went swiftly to the window, and, as cautiously as if he were a sniper trying to get a bead on an unsuspecting enemy, he imperceptibly parted the blind and looked out. "She's gone," he announced, his voice devoid of relief or triumph. It was simply a flat statement.

"How do you know it was your wife?" Gloria inquired idly, putting her hands behind her head and crossing her feet.

"Look, sweetie," he said by way of answer, "do you mind awfully if we skip dinner together? Here," he said, gathering up some bills from the bureau, "you go blow yourself to a nice meal, and I'll—I'll make it up to you later."

"What do you take me for?" she demanded in a surly voice, giving the age-old question no memorable change in tone value or sensitivity. Already, in fact, she was getting up, the bills accepted from his extended hand, even as she reached with the other for her clothes. She dressed silently, and Ernie didn't even bother to observe whether she did so in a continued show of pique or tart-like acceptance; he was too busy with his resumed sentinel duty at the window.

When she was ready to go, he seemed to sense it, and turned. "Good-bye, Gloria. Have a nice dinner. I'm sorry about all this."

She shrugged. "It don't matter, Ernie. But just call me sooner next time, will you?"

"Yes, I will," he promised, and let her out the door.

The first thing he did, of course, was shower. He grimaced as he soaped off the guilt-fear sweat, and the stains of Gloria's lovemaking, and asked himself again as he had repeatedly since the ringing of the bell whether his caller had been Joan or Peggy or, conceivably, somebody else entirely. Would he ever know? He had a feeling he would.

As he dried himself he noticed in the mirror that he could do with a shave. But for what? Was he going out? Was someone coming in? Thanks to Gloria, his whole evening had been disrupted, and he had treated her miserably, too. Before he had always prided himself upon the delicacy and pains he took to make such creatures feel not only wanted, but like ladies, and human beings as well. And here he had treated her just exactly like a whore— or as he imagined whores were treated by paying customers. He had never been a customer, although he had known his share of prostitutes: he had always, eternally—and to everybody—been a boyfriend.

Reasoning that he would probably go out for something to eat in any case, even if it were just to Billy's on First for a hamburger, he decided to shave. That over with, he stopped his toilette preparations to think. Suppose she—whoever it was—returned? Wouldn't it be better, in answering the door, to pretend he had been having a nap, preparatory to working on his report and a quiet can of soup or something? That way they wouldn't even have to go out. Another twenty or thirty bucks saved. But, he thought to himself, as he was knotting the sash on the handsome brocade dressing gown Angeline had given him two Christmases ago, I really am tired—up to here with sex—

It was then that he heard the key scratching at the lock, trying gently, unobtrusively, to fit itself in without too much noise. And once more his body went into paralysis; everything about him stunned and stopped except the short hair at the back of his neck.

As he stood unmoving in the darkened bedroom, one hand still on the once-looped sash, he thought, All right, Peggy, my girl, just you come in that door ... invade my privacy, victimize me with that key I was stupid enough to put in your hot little hand ... and catch me redhanded. He had the speech fully prepared; what a riot act he would read *her,* beginning with a scathing reminder that he would have telephoned her if he had wanted to see her; he would have told her if he had wanted her to know he was going to be in town, and FOR CHRIST'S SAKE STAY OUT OF HIS BUSINESS! GET OFF HIS BACK! Anger flared his nostrils as he moved noiselessly from the bedroom to the hall, the better to confront her as she opened the door, and, breathing hard, but making no tell-tale sign of so doing, he stared at the lock, listened to the key at last fitting in. Any minute now there would be a click as the lock turned, then she would open the door.

He waited and watched, breath now held. As she came in, he had decided, he'd give her one look, turn and walk into the living room. She could then follow, or back out, as she chose. But in amazement he realized she was having trouble with the lock. The tumbler was turning over and over; he could hear it, but nothing was happening. She wasn't turning the handle sharply enough, he was thinking. Once before, in fact the only time before, the night he had given her the key and they were trying it out, she had had trouble. And he had showed her how to work it. Though it was tricky, he had to admit. Now, sweetie, he thought, now when you hear that turning sound, twist the handle. But instead the tumbler continued to turn, over and over, again and again. You couldn't say she wasn't trying, he thought despondently.

To overcome his own nervousness he tiptoed away from the door, back into the bedroom. Anyway, when she finally did get that damned lock open, wouldn't it be better if he were coming from that direction to meet her, switching on lights, rather than be hovering behind the hall door in the dark? He strode toward the window to wait for the operation to be completed. He peered once more through the blind. Not quite dark yet, but street lights were on.

It was some time before he realized the noise at the lock had stopped and if she hadn't crossed the street, looked across once at his darkened windows, he might never have known that it had been she, Peggy.

In an unaccountable frenzy, he pulled the cord of the Venetian blind, sending it clattering up, and tugged at the partially opened window. "Peggy!" he called out into the dusk. "Peggy! Peggy!" But by that time she was too far away to hear.

He rushed to dress as if he were catching a train. God! What had he been thinking of? Why had he behaved like that? Why hadn't he opened the door when he heard the key in the lock, for who else had a key? Whom else did he want to have a key? She hadn't asked for it—he'd given it. So why shouldn't she use it? I'm crazy, crazy, crazy, he told himself as he hurriedly fastened his wristwatch on his arm. Then he saw it, lying face down on the floor by the bureau: the little circlet of Mexican silver he had bought her more or less as a joke when they were on the Coast. Tenderly, he picked it up, righting its face, the inscription on its plaque: To Peggy from the Swine. He hurled it across the room and fell over their bed—his and Peggy's—sobbing as if his heart would literally break. The sobs actually hurt him, they were so deep, as they lunged up and out of his raw throat, pummeling his ribs.

When at last he could control them, he lay on his back, stared at the ceiling, his chest heaving. Poor thing, she had come back for her bracelet. Of course it had been she who had been so busy on the telephone, with all the calls he had not answered, but she wouldn't have come back—not even for the bracelet—if she had thought she were interrupting anything. Peggy was far too cool and wise for that. No hot-headed Joan she, no pregnant cheating bitch! No, Peggy was true-blue. If she loved a man, she loved a human being, not a set of genitalia with those all important testes inconveniently located in the center of the body! He leapt from the bed, switched on the lamp and picked up the telephone.

It was picked up on the second ring, but in his tender urgency, it was Ernie's voice that spoke first. "Peggy—"

"No," said a male voice at the other end. "She isn't in."

Ernie frowned. "Have I the right number? I'm calling Mrs. Grannis."

"She isn't in," the voice repeated in a manner and accent as clipped as Ernie's own, not unlike his own. "However, this is her husband, and if you'd care to leave a message—"

CHAPTER THIRTY-FIVE

"SO, I MIGHT as well give myself up," Peggy gulped bravely, smiling through her tears, even though the phone was her only visual audience.

Giving herself up meant, of course, going to her apartment and confronting Tom—if he was there—and his quite justified anger, hurt, and bafflement. And now Bill Roche, who, as soon as he had realized her state, had gone into the bedroom to take her call on the extension for privacy's sake, advised her to do just that.

"Don't worry about a thing, hon," he said reassuringly again. "Now just you collect yourself and forget all about Ernie. As you say, he was a summer mistake and summer's over. You've got much more serious things to think about." He didn't add, as he would have thoroughly liked to have done, that Ernie was a first-class cad and he hoped Tom Grannis would take the horse whip to him before he was finished. For Ernie, devil-may-care, lady killer that he might fancy himself, had, if what Peggy had to say was true, and he had never had cause to doubt her word, gone, this time, much too far, as the saying goes.

Of course, he, Bill, had had his suspicions about what had been going on. Recently at lunch, Ernie's elaborate presentation of Peggy's name—not just the usual dropping it and toeing it along he customarily went in for when implying amorous connections—coupled with accounts of social doings in high quarters, indicated to Bill that something definitely was afoot and that Ernie was almighty pleased about it. Ernie had practically stood up on his hind legs and begged Bill to ask him to tell all, but Bill hadn't wanted to know. He still didn't.

He listened tiredly to Peggy's wind-up, his telephone ear feeling sticky and rather numb.

"Don't keep wiggling this business like a sore tooth," he advised. "All right, so you ran out on Tom and then you went there. And you saw this gal coming out of Ernie's apartment, and then you tried to get in with your key. So maybe you shouldn't have done it, but you did. And now you know."

"But I left my bracelet there," she said in a small voice.

"What's a bracelet?" Bill asked her harshly, out of kindness. "So it was an Ernie keepsake, a remembrance of things past. Is it really anything you want to keep?"

"No," Peggy said, her voice smaller than ever, and again thready with sobs. "I know I've said it before," she apologized, "but I shouldn't be burdening you with all this—especially at this late date."

"Forget about it," he said blandly. "Look, kid, you just go home. See Tom. Have yourself some dinner and a nice hot bath and bed and take it from there tomorrow."

"I guess you're right," she sobbed.

"I know I'm right," he said staunchly. "Ernie's not worth it— not nearly. And you should be glad you found out what a liar and a cheat, what an unhappy, miserable human being of a cheat he is, before you were involved further."

"Good night, Bill, and thanks a lot. I hope your dinner isn't completely cold."

"I'm sure it isn't irreparable in any case," he said. "Good night, kid, and give me a call tomorrow if you feel like it."

At last he was able to hang up. He sat there on the side of the bed feeling like old Dog Tray. Dejected was the word for it. Even his hands were hanging between his legs, and his shoulders were drooping, and so was his head. Snap out of it, Roche, he told himself. You've got your dinner to eat, and your children to chastise for that broccoli-throwing episode, and your wife to lend false comfort to for finding herself in that delicate condition which both of us want to find her in.... The cares of the world, Peggy being taken care of, would just have to wait. Now's the time for that charity at home.

He returned to the living room. Alice was serving dessert on the card table from which they had dined: the dining table being occupied at the moment by a number of inedibles consisting of some crockery Joan had bought at auction; his discarded socks and some shirts from which Kathy was to make a rag rug for her class project; a pile of old papers which he hoped did not include any of his precious notes, so carefully guarded, for the Eakins book; a pair of large hedge shears, mistakenly brought in from the country, and various and sundry his eye failed to put name to in its roving identification. In any event, the dining table was eminently unfit for dining this night, and the card table, while a trifle intimate (downright cramped) had seen them through thus far. And, once dessert was over—gobbled through, in all probability—and the children steered, urged and re-steered off to their separate bedrooms, Alice would serve coffee in the living room, properly, and the amenities could once more be observed.

For some reason this took less time to accomplish than usual; though, of course, Bill was aware that he had helped matters along by not protesting that Alice had removed his plate, virtually untouched, piled high as it had been with mouth-watering fried chicken. Instead, he made do with his chocolate pudding, like a good boy.

"Seconds, dear?" Joan asked in mild surprise as he held out his dessert plate. She scooped a scant two spoonfuls in, as the children adored chocolate pudding, and, after all, Bill had his growth. "You must have had a hard day at the office. Who was that who just now called?"

"Our problem child," he said with a sigh.

Joan gave a faint sniff of disdain. "Oh, *her*. What does she want now?"

Bill did not immediately answer, sensing as he did that there had been a sudden and radical change of wind in that department, and the barometer had fallen like there was a leak in it somewhere. "Tom's back," he said at last, and pointedly reached over for the chocolate pudding bowl to help himself.

"Well, I'm glad," said Joan. "Maybe it will steady her."

"Or unsteady her completely," Bill remarked dryly.

Joan made a gesture of disinterest. Then cried, "Children! no more television! I mean that, Billy. Turn it off this minute and go put on your pajamas!"

Bill smirked at her slightly, before applying himself to more of his purloined pudding.

"All right!" she said. "You may laugh, but you know perfectly well that if I don't start now they'll never go to bed."

"Why not let Eunuch, or Eunice, or whatever her name is take care of that? After all, that was what she was hired for, wasn't it? As far as I can tell, after eight she takes up her sideline with the lumber yard."

"What do you mean?"

"I mean, my dear wife," he said caustically, "that she lies in her room and saws logs while you and I sit out here and make like a pair of inexpert babysitters pressed into service for free."

"Well, you son-of-a-bitch," she said matter-of-factly, looking him over calmly, as detached and determined upon judging as if it were the first viewing.

"Son-of-a-bitch, son-of-a-bitch," he repeated with a gesture and ate some more. "Even Alice could get them to bed without all this folderol. She did in the country."

"Well, you weren't on the phone all the time out there with some problem-ridden babe!"

He looked into her fury with a cold eye; a knowing, if not a telling eye. "Where did you pick up that 'babe' expression?" he asked casually, applying himself to his food again.

"What? I don't know what you're talking about!"

He sighed, stood up. "Do you think Alice has persuaded the coffee to drip through yet, or are we having instant?" he asked.

"You and your sarcasm!" she exclaimed. "Of course we're having real coffee, just as we always do! You may think I'm a slob, that I run my house that way, but you're wrong! I give every bit as good as I get! I'm not on the phone—or at lunch—or having cocktails—with every woebegone, threadbare—"

At that moment, Alice, with unusual dignity, entered the living room, and, with some pomp, to match her expression and her crisp uniform, laid the coffee things, the liqueurs and glasses, at the proper place; her hauteur saying, as she turned her back, they can fight all they pleases; *I'se* done my duty.

Bill, as he filled the cups, filled the glasses, smiled to himself, having gotten all this. But Joan, still in a faraway storm-tossed area of thunder and lightning, came down on him. "What's so funny?" she demanded.

"Nothing, dear," he said mildly.

"God," she muttered, lifting her cup to sip her coffee, "sometimes I hate you."

"Do you, dear?"

"Yes, I do, *dear*," she underlined the word. "I hate you for your so-called Big Heart, for listening to everybody's troubles—"

"—I listen to yours," he interrupted.

She gave an abrupt, short-lived laugh, hollow as a death rattle. "But since I met you, Bill Roche, I haven't *had* any troubles." Delivered of this, she put her head back on the couch and laughed and laughed.

Bill watched her in a mixture of curiosity and apprehension: she had had maybe three drinks before dinner—maybe more, if the at-home ones had quickly followed those she had had out at some cocktail bar with a shopping friend, as she had said. But, all the same, it was not exactly nerving to see them hit her like this. Yes, something else besides drink and discovery of her state of coming motherhood was responsible. She was too loose-jointed, too abandoned, too ready for anything tonight. "Joan," he said evenly, "why are you so unsettled? Has something I don't know about upset you?"

"No!" she cried out vigorously and seemed ready to stamp her foot at him.

"Are you angry at me then?" he asked mildly.

"Of course I'm angry at you," she said, her speech thickening. "You're always letting that Peggy bitch con you."

"Con me? Con me how?"

"Into being her patsy!" Joan told him heatedly. "You talked to her four hours on the telephone when you should have been eating your dinner."

"I didn't talk to her 'four hours,' " he quoted acidly. "I didn't even talk to her one. As a matter of fact, my love, I talked to her just long enough for you to tell Alice to clear the table even though I had just begun my food."

Joan burst into a blind thicket of sobs at this cruelty and started to leave the room, but Bill's sense of justice was aroused. "Just a minute there," he said and rather roughly assisted her back into a sitting position on the couch. This is not my night for senseless scenes, Joan, and I'm not going to let you get away with this business this time. Just you sit up there like a good girl and tell me why all of a sudden you've taken it into your head to get so loaded, number one, nasty, number two, and resentful about Peggy, number three. You seem to overlook the fact that she's also a friend of yours."

Joan gave him a hazy faraway smile. "Billy said the cutest thing today. He said there was a little boy in his class who was mean enough to pull the wings off airplanes."

"Now isn't that just adorable?" Bill commented, staring at his wife and wondering if pregnancy and drink had permanently affected her mind. "But suppose you answer my three-part question."

CHAPTER THIRTY-SIX

IRST JOAN tried the old ploy of, "What question?" but Bill's patience was too far spent to endure any mock innocence at this point, so pinned down, she said with a sigh, "Well, it's a long story," to which he replied that he had plenty of time. Then, hedging still further, she said, "Suppose you tell me first what Peggy was so worked up about now that Tom's returned? Did he take an axe to her at the airport?"

"That really isn't very funny," Bill answered, "and I don't know why you're being so evasive with me, but if it will help you collect your thoughts any I'll tell you what Peggy said. It seems she saw Tom just long enough to wave to him then simply hauled herself off, into a taxi, and back to the city, leaving the poor bastard to do and think whatever he liked."

"But that's insane!" Joan exclaimed.

"I'll agree that it isn't quite normal," Bill said dryly.

"And so, of course, she called you, Dr. Freud, to find out if you could dig up any explanation from that mire of an unconscious of hers for having done such a thing."

"No, my sweet and charitable wife, she had already uprooted that hot potato."

"What was the hot potato, as you call it?"

He eyed her thoughtfully. "I'm not sure I should tell you—now or at any other time. You've got your dander up about Peggy for some reason, and what she told me was very private indeed—so private that I'm not sure she should have told me, of all people."

Joan, who appeared to have sobered somewhat, gave a sigh. "Well, what you've done, of course, is hopelessly stimulate my curiosity. I needn't tell you that's not fair."

"No, you needn't. I know it, and I'm sorry."

"Won't you even give me a hint? You know, Bill, that I really like Peggy very much, that I haven't a hostile bone in my body. It was just that I heard something today—and don't ask me who told me; I have my secrets, too—that shocked and distressed me. I had never thought Peggy capable of underhandedness."

"What did you hear?" he asked suspiciously.

"That Peggy and Ernie actually did have an affair that week-end they spent with us and that it's been going on hot and heavy ever since." She delivered this brilliant extemporaneous lie with masterly insouciance and closely watched Bill for its effect.

The effect was immediate and resounded like a shot. "Good grief!" he exclaimed. "I don't know which of your gossip mongers let fly with that, but it certainly means that poor Peggy has by no means been as discreet as she thought."

"You mean it's true?" Joan gasped in amazement. "How could it be true?"

"Certainly, it's true," he replied abruptly, frowning at her. "You found it perfectly acceptable as true when you picked it off the grapevine—'shocked and distressed'; isn't that what you said you were?"

"You mean she actually *told* you herself that this was what's been going on?" she persisted disbelievingly. "That slut! Fouling my house, and with my innocent young children—!"

"Look here, Queen Victoria," he said in open scorn, "you seem to be forgetting a few moral items about yourself, told to me not without a touch of pride, I might add, and a few little illicit escapades involving myself—"

"But that was before I was married!" she protested. And then she made the awful mistake of blushing, literally to the roots of her hair, and the blush stood there for what seemed to both of them an eternity, as telling as the scarlet letter. She looked down at her hands.

"Well, since you blushed so prettily, you've left me no alternative but to question your guilt. Have you been unfaithful to me, my wife?"

"Of course not!" she said angrily and reached over for her brandy snifter, knocking over the sugar bowl.

"Good God, Joan, if I didn't know better, I'd swear you'd turned me into a Texas longhorn, many times over, judging from your rattled state."

"Oh, you crazy fool!" she cried at him, tears glistening on her cheeks. "Must you think every married woman is going to behave like Peggy? The whole thing just makes me furious. Poor Tom. I think someone should tell him."

"Someone like you, perhaps?" he asked with icy calm.

"No. Someone like you."

He shook his head sternly. "No, Joan. Not you, not me. Not nobody, as far as I'm concerned. That's their problem, not ours, and anyway, knowing Peggy, I rather imagine she'll tell him herself—"

"*Knowing* Peggy!" Joan repeated, fairly scorching the words. "While we're on the subject, my fine husband, just how well do you know Peggy, if you get what I mean!"

"You're drunk and you're very disgusting," he said rising from his chair.

"Oh, am I?" she shrieked. "It's all right for you to accuse me, but it's drunk and disgusting when I accuse you!"

"Okay, honey," he said, "but I didn't blush."

"And you didn't answer the question either!" she blazed on.

"All right, kiddo. You asked for it," he said standing with his hands on the back of the chair, his eyes boring into hers. "No. I have never been unfaithful to you with Peggy, not that I would have minded. Not that I would mind right now, seeing as how you're so delectable and sweet-tempered at the moment—"

"You—you—!" she spluttered and jumped up and began to claw at him, at his face, his chest, his ears.

When she tore his shirt he put her away from him firmly, walked to the hall closet, took down his hat, and walked out the front door.

CHAPTER THIRTY-SEVEN

"OH," SAID Ernie in bald-faced disappointment, "it's you."

"Yes, it is," Joan admitted meekly, trying not to sniffle too loudly into the telephone. "Ernie, something just dreadful has happened—is there any chance that your date, Gloria—that is, could you possibly get away for a few minutes and meet me, darling? Say at that place on your corner, Fanny's, or whatever it's—?"

"No, not Fanny's," he said emphatically, his voice still cold as ice. "But I'm alone. You can come here."

"Oh, thank God!" she cried in glad relief.

"What's the matter?" his voice now scornful, as well as cold. "Did you have a miscarriage or something?"

"What an awful thing to joke about, Ernie," she reproved him. "But no, it's not about the baby. It's something else."

It had better be good, he thought as he told her good-bye and hung up. Because he was in a black mood; so black that he wasn't even sure he wanted to see the one person he wanted to see. He kept telling himself that somehow it would all work out all right. Even if Tom was back, so what? The chances were—especially now—that Tom would just leave again. For what man wants to live with a woman who is in love with some other guy? Money, advantages, et cetera notwithstanding, who could take that sort of punishment to pride and manhood?

The minute Ernie opened the door he knew by the way she stood that she was drunk. What he did not know was that after

Bill had walked out on her Joan had laced her courage for her call to Ernie with several gulped snifters of brandy, and had fortified herself for the trip with still more. In fact, she was so drunk that she didn't appear to know where she was, or how she'd gotten there.

And as they walked into the living room and sat down, it became apparent to Ernie that she had also lost track of the reason why she had come. She immediately grasped his hand and began to fondle it, cooing over it, and pressing it to her tear-streaked cheeks. Ernie removed himself.

"My, you're looking lovely tonight," he remarked with insulting sarcasm.

"Am I?" she asked in a daze.

"Yes, so well that I think you'd better go home. Right now."

She shook her head, and continued to wobble it from side to side after her point was made, as if she either liked it that way or couldn't stop herself.

"Yes, sweetie, I'll see you to a cab," he said, and started for the closet to hastily reattire himself.

"Speckinher, I know," Joan mumbled so drunkenly that he had to ask her what she had said. "Specking her, is what I said!" she cried at him, momentarily revivified by anger.

"No," he said stiffly. "Gloria is not expected."

"But Peggy-pot is, am I right?" she said thickly, trying to focus her eyes on his face.

"Are you always such a possessive, suspicious bitch, or have you been saving it all up for me?" he demanded, quite furious at her surprising accusation.

"So you are specting her," Joan murmured glumly, as if to herself.

"Come on," he said taking her limp hand, trying to get her on her feet.

"Not going," said Joan stubbornly. "Gonna stay and scratch her eyes out. She's stolen my man."

Ernie called her an exceedingly filthy name, surprising himself. He had never addressed a woman in such terms before. Having done so, he became even more coldly furious, as if Joan had brought him to this. However, Joan did not seem to notice. Instead she continued her mumbling accusations against Peggy, though oddly enough, not against Ernie.

"Trying to steal the father of my unborn child," she mouthed. "I'll fix her."

Ernie slapped her soundly across the face. "Shut your filthy mouth!" he screamed at her, trembling, frightened, furious. "Take yourself out of here. Get out of my house and out of my life!"

"You love her better than you do me," Joan pouted sleepily, feeling her wounded face, seemingly unaware of why it hurt.

"I don't love you at all! I despise you!" Now he was tugging at her, trying to haul her away.

She struggled loosely to stay where she was, but was too weak and sodden with drink to hold her ground. Ernie was pushing her, yanking her toward the door. Somehow he managed to get it open and pushed her outside. Then, finding her purse where it had fallen on the floor, he swiftly went back and threw it after her. She was lying in the hallway, her skirts up to her thighs, exposing her fleshy white legs where the stockings left off.

Shaking all over, he returned to the living room and sat heavily on the couch. Then he picked up his unfinished drink, trying to steady his hand, trying to steady his wits, get his bearings.

It had all happened with such ferocious and confusing suddenness that he could not comprehend it; he sat in a near state of shock as if he had, moments before, been in a violent traffic accident and was now surrounded by the dead. How had Peggy gotten into all this, and had Joan come here for the purpose of confronting her? Had Tom somehow learned about what had been going on while he was away? Had Peggy gone to cry on the Roche's shoulders? Who, why, when, what, how? The answers absolutely evaded him. He had been so careful, so tactful, so adroit. Why had everything gone suddenly wild like a cyclotron, exploding, spewing out disaster everywhere?

Then suddenly he got to his feet and went to the front door and peered out. He could not leave Joan permanently lying in the hall like that. This was a respectable, quiet house, and she had collapsed just outside his door. At first he didn't see her, and he felt both panic and relief. Anything to get rid of her, but not in a way that would implicate him. But she had not staggered off into the night or been discovered by the superintendent and taken away: she was sitting on the stairs leading to the second floor, holding her face and weeping softly. He saw that her hand was covered with blood, and that the blood was streaming from a cut on her face which she had undoubtedly gotten when he pushed her out and she had fallen. What a bloody mess! he thought.

"Come in here, Joan," he commanded crisply.

She looked up, then looked away and her sobbing became wracked and gasping, as if she were about to choke.

Fixing the nightlatch so he would not lock himself out, he went out into the hall and gathered her up, but she was almost a dead weight. He could not carry her and she refused to walk, so he dragged her across the hall, her lifeless legs trailing along. Once he got her inside the door, he tried to prop her up, but she fell, so he left her to go back and retrieve her purse and one shoe which had fallen off in passage.

He glared at her as she lay on the floor; now she was completely passed out and snoring. His nausea drained the blood from his face. "Jesus God!" he muttered in outrage and contempt and returned to the living room, leaving her where she was. How to get her out of the place, and where to? He couldn't very well call up Bill to come collect his filthy baggage. And he certainly couldn't leave her here, and he was certainly not going to hang around, wait for her to sober up and start her nagging and implications about Peggy all over again. It was none of her God damned business, and he wanted her out of his sight—out of his life—as quickly as possible, unborn child or no unborn child. Anyway, that was probably just one of her tricks to entice him into going to bed with her again, on a more or less regular basis as he had foolishly let himself promise her back in the summer before he realized how serious she was, and how much of a threat she was to his privacy—maybe, even to his marriage; with a vicious bitch like Joan, you never knew how far they would go.

At the thought of Betsy being apprized of all of this—if she had not been already—he felt a sharp turning chill in his solar plexus. Betsy! Oh, no. That couldn't happen. He must not let Joan get to Betsy!

Though it was now after ten o'clock and Betsy was an early retirer, he went to the telephone and dialed their Montclair number. The telephone rang and rang. Damn, he thought, she must have turned it off; she did that sometimes as she didn't sleep well. Just to make sure he hadn't been calling the wrong number, he dialed the operator and had her place the call, but he had no better luck this time. Betsy simply wasn't answering the phone. There was a remote chance, of course, that she was out playing bridge, or maybe this was one of the PTA nights. But whatever, now Ernie knew he had to go out there tonight and talk to her. What would he say? He didn't know. If she heard that it was Peggy, not to mention Joan (what a thought!) she wouldn't take to it kindly; before he had always confined his amorous interests to women outside their circle of friends. On the way out he would think of something. But first he had to dispose of the body, so to speak.

He considered simply taking her with him to the station and dumping her inert in the waiting room, leaving her to sleep it off there. But that might get him into deep trouble—even with the police. It was a far too conspicuous thing to do. But he certainly could not leave her here to recover—suppose, for instance, Peggy sneaked a chance to phone him, and Joan, of course, would answer the phone; it was just the kind of opportunity she would crave. Or, if Betsy called—oh, anybody. No. He could not leave her here anymore than he could unload her at her own home. Too many explanations to be offered; too many doormen; too much everything.

Then the solution came to him. Charlotte Adams! Good ole Charlie would take over, and Hank could help him manage her into their apartment. And, maybe, Ernie thought with malicious pleasure, Hank might even reward himself for his efforts, as soon as Joan returned a little more to the land of the living. He, Ernie, could certainly recommend her charms, and, moreover, if she were really knocked up, she was as safe as a neuter.

Once again he picked up the phone and called Charlotte.

CHAPTER THIRTY-EIGHT

CHARLOTTE WAS a little under the weather herself, it appeared as she let them into the apartment, and gave him a wide hooded-eyed grin and a yawn for which she apologized as he and his burden made their way over the threshold. "Sleepy," she explained. "Was having a little nap."

She showed Ernie the bedroom where he could stash Joan, and, having done so, they both began to get her partially undressed, so she could rest more comfortably. This was Charlotte's idea, and he snorted at it scornfully. "I should have put her in a gutter under ten feet of water," he remarked.

Charlotte giggled, and they returned to the living room. "You want to stay here tonight?" she asked him, yawning again.

"I wouldn't spend the night under the same roof with that one for a fortune," he promised in a steely voice.

Charlotte laughed languidly and waved a hand. "That bad, huh?" she asked. "Well, you can share my bed, baby."

Ernie shook his head. "Love you as I do, Charlie, I've had it for today. "Anyway, where's ole Hank? Three in a bed isn't too comfortable for long-range arrangements."

"It would just be the two of us tonight, baby," she said, but she was by no means insisting. "Hank's out."

"Oh?" said Ernie with curiosity. "Got a new number? And what is it this time, boy or girl?"

Charlotte gave him her goodnatured laugh again. "Girl, honey, and you damned well know it. And not new either. Something he's had going for some time."

"A real swinging thing, to quote your vernacular, huh?" he asked, and added, "Why aren't you jealous? Everybody *I* know is jealous—except you."

"Well, I am, too, in a way. Only his hang-up with this one is now old and comfortable, and I don't think it can go any further than it's gone. I mean, I think they are both satisfied with the way things stand."

"You mean she knows you know?"

"Certainly," she assured him with a nod. "It works out very well because it's a sort of a swap. I occasionally go to bed with hers and she goes to bed with mine."

"Sounds delicious and fascinating. Why haven't you confessed all this before?"

She gave him a lazy shrug. "Oh," she said, "reasons. And then, too, it's not all that constant any more. And besides her husband doesn't know—though he would if he had eyes in his head—but he's terribly possessive and jealous."

"Sounds like me," he said with a smirk.

"You've got your similarities," she agreed. "Nice ones. Sure you don't want to stay over tonight."

"Now, Charlie," he said with a nervous laugh.

"All right, all right," she said, laughing back. "But do tell me what you want done with Madame Roche."

"Oh, call up Bill later and tell him to come collect her. But wait until she's sobered up enough to talk to her. I don't want her blabbing all kinds of nonsense to him, accusing me of all manner of things—"

"Just what could she accuse you of?" Charlotte queried. "You know I'm completely in the dark about this whole take. All I know is what you told me on the phone: that she turned up at your place drunk and disorderly, which seemed rather surprising to me in itself. Do you two have something going? And what's happened to Peggy, or were you telling the truth last month when you said that had dwindled off to nothing and you had something else on the horizon?"

Ernie sighed. "I guess I'd better fill you in a bit," he said. "Not that the whole dreary business is of much interest, but *she*—" he nodded toward the room where Joan was sleeping—"will be giving you an earful, and you might as well have the facts."

Charlotte gave a loud amiable laugh at this ludicrous thought: Ernie, as they both perfectly knew, was incapable of rendering the facts. However.... And he proceeded to "fill her in," deftly skipping about here and there among the past events, editing some, totally obscuring others that he thought she might not come across or in some way notice. When he was finished, having also finished his third drink, he stood up and said he thought it was time to go. These night-time flurries of passion and hate still did not obliterate the necessity of returning to the business world tomorrow.

"I truly admire you, Ernie," Charlotte said at the door. "You've got your whole life divided into the most convenient compartments. You're lucky they don't spill over more often."

He kissed her lightly on the mouth and patted her arm. "That's because I'm not a slob," he said acknowledging the compliment. "I keep my house all nice and neat; everything in its place; everything in order."

"And what they don't know won't hurt 'em," she called after him as if this observation were a witticism.

"That's right," he called back. "Go to bed and don't sleep too tight now."

"Okay," she said. "I'll call you later if I run into any trouble with Sleeping Ugly."

He paused, on the verge of telling her he wouldn't be staying in town tonight, then called, "Do that." He couldn't run the risk of brash Charlotte calling him out in Montclair about these matters. She was like a beautiful woman with no sense of modesty, and taking one's clothes off just any old where could cause a lot of trouble.

CHAPTER THIRTY-NINE

O N THE train, Ernie realized how much this awful day had taken out of him, but there wasn't really time for a nap, and his eye really did hurt him this time so he couldn't read. Then too, the obvious reading material, his report, he had, of course, left in the apartment since he had had both hands busy dragging Joan out.

What a mess she was, and how lucky he was not to be Bill Roche! Especially now with this pregnancy thing. All the joy of second-hand fatherhood had left him. He hoped, as a matter of fact, that she would abort, or that the kid would be born dead, or something lucky, for Joan wasn't fit to be a mother, of any child, much less his. But what he couldn't figure out was how she'd tumbled to this Peggy bit. Somebody had told something, or seen something, and Joan had been on to it in a flash. Then it occurred to him that Joan had been too drunk to do more than mumble about Peggy. What had been her intention in coming to him? On the phone, before coherence left her, she had said something dreadful had happened, or words to that effect? Could she, in her terrible romantic fancy, have somehow decided that she should leave Bill and move herself and her oncoming bundle of joy in on him? Ernie shuddered. He had to admit that with her such a catastrophe was more than a possibility. And the more he thought about it, the more he was inclined to think that was the answer. For if she hadn't walked out on Bill, leaving Bill for him, what could she have been thinking of? Bill wouldn't have let her go off so drunk and so late at night if there hadn't been some sort of scene between them. Oh, God! Ernie muttered to himself and wished that the train would just go faster. Well, he knew how to fix Joan, squelch her manipulations. It was easy enough just to give up the apartment and move back home with Betsy—if he got to Betsy first, before Joan or others had time to do their mindpoisoning. Sometimes he wasn't even sure he could trust old Charlotte and Hank with all they knew—and had gone through. Well, all he could do was try. He had no doubt of Betsy's understanding, though he had some reason to trust to her total tolerance, regardless of how he rendered the facts to her, how circumspectly he behaved.

Then, too, there was the sad matter of really having to give up Peggy if he moved back home. Since her husband had returned there would be no trysting place, at least until she got rid of him, and trying to keep up that sort of thing—at best— with sharp-eyed Betsy would put him under a difficult strain. As if it were already over for months, he looked back upon their old life together—his and Peggy's—with nostalgia as strong as though it had not skipped the first stage of real grief. But, he told himself, it would be better this way in the long run; taking cover with Betsy. And, besides, there was always next year, and there were always more babes. Eventually, no matter what happened, he knew that he would have had to break with Peggy. She was no lifetime project, as Betsy was. In fact, he perfectly well knew that Betsy was his only lifetime project. Though it would have been nice to be in Europe with Peggy, on her money. However, he yawned, as he summarized the whole thing to himself, all was by no means finished, polished off; many ifs, ands, and buts could again change the whole picture. But he did think that the best thing he could do for the time being was return to Montclair and give up the pleasant little place in town. Betsy, as he had many times discovered in the past, was his Rock of Gibraltar—though, of course, he had never let her know how completely this was true. It was ruinous with women to let them know how dependent a man can be upon them. His steadfast Betsy who docilely stood by, shutting her eyes to the way he managed his life and affairs, was always there; his, the mother of his children, abiding, cool and serene.

When he got off the train there were no taxis in sight, but regardless of what the night had been in New York, out here it was quiet, dark, pleasant. He decided to walk home, even though it was a long walk and he would have to get an especially early start in the morning to get to his apartment, get things collected there, and reach the office in time. And tomorrow he would try to call Peggy, find out what was what with her renewed marriage, and sorrowfully break it to her that he felt he must return to Montclair. He would use the old thing about how Betsy was not taking proper care of the children; was letting the house fall to pieces, etcetera, etcetera. Not that there wasn't in it some basis of truth. Betsy was an indifferent housekeeper and was perhaps too permissive as a mother, but it was nothing fatal.

As he walked along, he felt peace descending on him like a soft cloak; relaxation seeped into his marrow as if he had had an injection of some sort. If commuting weren't such a bother and if life in the suburbs weren't such a bore, and if he could ever be satisfied with just one babe year in and year out, this life would be matchless. But one had to face reality; it wasn't. He, like everyone else, had to satsfy himself with compromise.

He turned into the gate at his house and the children's dog, who slept on the porch until actual winter began, barked at him as if he were a stranger. But then he practically was; besides, he disliked dogs and secretly feared them. He got the dog quieted and noticed that the house was completely dark. He opened the door and walked inside, not tiptoeing, but being careful to make no noise. Everybody would have long since been asleep.

Cautiously, he turned on the living room light and went directly to the kitchen to fix himself a drink. When he returned he saw empty glasses on the coffee table, and unfilled ice trays carelessly lying about. Betsy had apparently been entertaining. Maybe she would like to wake up and have a drink too. On this assumption, he returned to the kitchen, finally washed a glass and filled it, finding no clean ones, and came back. He turned on the stairway light and hesitated. Maybe it would be better if he slept in the guestroom and left her a note saying he was here. He didn't like to disturb her; might frighten her. Only on two or three other occasions during their marriage had he ever returned home unexpected, unannounced, and on one of these he knew he had given her quite a start.

Well, he decided, he would just have to run that risk—so would she—for he needed her tonight, needed someone calm and pleasant and familiar to talk to—and, after all, what was a wife for? Moreover, he needed to feel her out on the subjects of Joan and Peggy, oil the waters, pave the way, or do whatever was needed to keep her on even keel.

He crept up the stairs, both drinks in hand, and stopped at the door to their bedroom. It was closed. Which meant he had probably been right about the phone having been shut off; she probably had one of her headaches. Once more, he was tempted just to let her sleep and take things up tomorrow. He didn't want to make her irritable; he'd had quite enough of female temper for one day. But all the same, he opened the door and felt around for the lamp with the dim bulb on the bureau. He switched it on.

Betsy lay in the bed, her long auburn hair unleashed against the whiteness of the pillow, a sweet smile on her face as she slept cradled in the still quite suntanned arms of Hank Adams.

Ernie stood there briefly, then he switched out the light, carried the two drinks back down the stairs to the living room, put them on the coffee table, hers beside his, and sat down.

Absently, he removed the eye patch from his eye and rubbed it. His eye was hurting him again. He picked up his drink and sipped it and made a face. Even liquor didn't taste right anymore.